Rough Riders of the Ragged Rimrock

Also by James J. Griffin and available from Center Point Large Print:

Tall Trouble in Terlingua
Catch a Falling Star
Death Comes to Lajitas
Change of Venue
Desperate Ride
Trouble Times Two
Ride for Justice, Ride for Revenge
Bullet for a Ranger
The Zombies of Zapata
The Ranger
To Avenge a Ranger
Murder Most Fowl—Texas Style

Rough Riders of the Ragged Rimrock

A Texas Ranger Will Kirkpatrick Novel

JAMES J. GRIFFIN

CENTER POINT LARGE PRINT
THORNDIKE, MAINE

This Center Point Large Print edition
is published in the year 2024 by arrangement with
the author.

Copyright © 2024 by James J. Griffin.

All rights reserved.

This is a work of fiction. Names, characters, places,
and incidents either are the product of the author's
imagination or are used fictitiously.
Any resemblance to actual persons, living or dead,
events, or locales is entirely coincidental.

The text of this Large Print edition is unabridged.
In other aspects, this book may vary
from the original edition.
Printed in the United States of America
on permanent paper sourced using
environmentally responsible foresting methods.
Set in 16-point Times New Roman type.

ISBN: 979-8-89164-306-2

The Library of Congress has cataloged this record
under Library of Congress Control Number: 2024940274

1

Seven men on horseback waited at the summit of a steep ridge. They were looking into the cut through which ran the road on which the weekly Dallas to Albuquerque stage would pass any time now. Scrub brush growing on the ridge hid them from the view of anyone passing down below.

"You've all got your assignments," Luke Trent, the gang's leader, said. "Any of you messes up and it'll be the last time. I'll personally gut-shoot you."

"We've pulled plenty of stage holdups, Luke," Pasco Lawton, his second-in-command, said. "The men know what to do."

A thin column of brown dust rising on the eastern horizon, staining the cloudless blue sky, marked the approach of the westbound stage. The cloud grew rapidly as the driver urged the six-horse team on at a gallop. The stage's next stop would be Sweetwater, about thirty miles distant.

"Masks up!" Trent ordered, "Smitty, you, Joe, and Hank get down there. The stage'll have to slow when it hits the grade, so you should have no trouble gettin' it to stop. The rest of you, get ready."

Smitty Smith nodded his acknowledgement. He and his two chosen partners pulled up their masks, then urged their horses over the edge of the sloping cut and down to the road. Trent and the rest of his men pulled bandanas over their faces, lowered their hats over their eyes, and lifted rifles from their scabbards. They were all mounted on dark horses, with no white markings to make them identifiable to any witnesses. Their saddles and bridles were also unadorned, and the men wore drab cowboy garb. It was highly unlikely anyone would be able to positively point out any of the gang as one of the men who had held up the stage. Not that Trent intended to leave anyone alive. Dead people couldn't testify in court. He'd gone by that rule his entire outlaw career, and it had served him well. He didn't intend to change his ways now.

Smitty, Joe Barnes, and Hank Dawkins were in place, just beyond the crest of the grade. The stage was now close enough they could hear the horses' pounding hooves, the shouts of the driver urging them on, the cracks of his whip, the rattling of the Concord and the creaking of its leather thoroughbraces.

By the time the stage reached the top of the grade, the horses were moving barely faster than a slow jogtrot. When the driver saw the three men blocking the road, rifles leveled at him and the shotgun guard, he knew his only choice was to stop. He hauled back on the reins. Wordlessly, the three men in the road opened fire, blasting the driver back in his seat, slumped dead. The guard had started to stand and aim his Greener, but the bullets ripping into him tore the life from his body. He sagged, then toppled sideward off his seat, landing in the road with a thump. From the top of the cut, the other outlaws poured a volley of lead into the stage, bullets ripping through the thin wooden panels and open windows, plowing into the luggage on the roof, shredding valises, carpetbags, and their contents. At a signal from Trent, the gunfire stopped. Silence descended, broken only by the twittering of nervous birds, the worried nickering of horses and the stamping of their hooves.

The men who had blocked the road walked their horses up to the stagecoach. Smith and Barnes looked inside, while Dawkins checked the driver and guard. Trent led the rest of his gang off the ridge and into the cut.

Smith yelled out in surprise when he looked through the coach's right-hand windows. There were three dead men. One wore a cheap suit and derby hat and held a blood-stained sample case. He appeared to be a drummer. The other two wore typical ranch hand clothing. Two more passengers were huddled on the floor, as far under the rear seat as they could squeeze.

"There's two people still alive inside. One of 'em's a woman."

"Get them outta there," Trent ordered.

Smith and Barnes got off their horses. They opened the right-side door and dragged the two survivors out. They were a young couple, apparently Easterners, both well dressed. The husband had evidently pushed his wife to the floor and lain on top of her, shielding her with his own body. He was bleeding copiously from a number of bullet wounds. His wife had only a graze on her right arm. Her blue eyes blazed defiantly at her captors, as she pushed a strand of her blonde hair back in place. She held her husband upright as he sagged against her for support.

"Hey Luke, we've got a real pretty young filly here," Smith said. When he reached out to touch the woman, she slapped him hard across his mouth, a hard enough blow to split his lips and knock out a front tooth.

"Don't you dare try and lay a hand on me again, you filthy pig!"

"Smitty, looks like you done just tangled with a wildcat," Trent said, laughing. Smith spit out the tooth and glared at his boss.

"She sure is a feisty one. A regular spitfire," Lawton added. "You reckon we should take her along with us, Luke?"

"That's a plumb stupid question, ya idjit," Trent answered. "Of course we're gonna take her along. A woman is the one thing this outfit's been missin'."

The woman stamped her right foot.

"I'm not going anywhere with you . . . you cretins!"

"Who's gonna stop us from doin' just that, bringin' you along, sweetheart?" Trent retorted. "All the men are dead, except your husband, and he ain't got long. I reckon we might just as well put him out of his misery now. It'd be a kindness to you. You won't have to watch him bleed out and die slow. Although mebbe I should let him suffer, because I don't know what you just called us, darlin', but I don't think I like it."

Trent aimed his gun at the young man's chest.

"Mister, I can't stop you from killing me," the Easterner gasped out. "I know I'm already mortally wounded as it is. But please, could I give Pamela just one last kiss before you shoot me down?"

Trent laughed cruelly.

"What's your name, *hombre*?"

"Phillip Hardy, from Baltimore, Maryland."

"Well, Mr. Phillip Hardy from Baltimore, Maryland, you don't need to worry about your sweet little wife getting kissed. She'll have plenty of kissin' and huggin' from me and the boys. Probably more than she ever got from you."

"Please, Mister, I'm begging you. If you have any honor, any decency, you'll allow me one final good-bye kiss with my wife."

Trent looked at his men.

"What do y'all think? Should we let this dude

have a last kiss with this sweet young thang?"

"He did ask awful purty-like," Lawton said. "What could it hurt? It might even warm her up a bit for us."

Trent nodded at Hardy.

"All right, go ahead, *hombre*. One kiss. But make it quick," Trent said. "We can't stick around here much longer. We'd purely hate to have to kill anyone else who happened along."

"Thank you."

Hardy turned his wife to face him and held her close. He slipped a two shot Derringer from inside his shirt sleeve, keeping it hidden in the palm of his hand.

"Remember what we agreed we'd do if anything like this happened?" he whispered.

"Yes," Pamela whispered back. "I love you."

"I love you too. We'll be in Heaven together, very soon."

Hardy pushed the snub-nosed little pistol against Pamela's chest, kissed her good-bye, and fired, putting a bullet into her heart. As she fell, he placed the Derringer against his right temple, cocked the hammer, and pulled the trigger, sending the remaining bullet into his brain. He fell alongside his wife. He'd committed murder, that of his own wife, then took his own life, but in doing so spared her being ravaged mercilessly by the outlaw gang, who would have, sooner or later, killed her anyway, or worse, sold her into slavery in Mexico once they were through with her. He'd also cheated them of the satisfaction of killing him.

"What the Hell just happened?" Smith yelled.

"That bastard tenderfoot outsmarted us, damn him. He had a hide-out gun. That's what happened. He spoiled our fun," Trent said. "Nothin' to be done about it now. Get the strongbox, bust it open, and load the contents into your saddlebags. Gather any valuables from the bodies, and stuff those in your pockets. Hurry. We've gotta vamoose. We've been here too long already."

Ten minutes later, the only signs of life in the cut were the stage horses, which Trent always left behind, the buzzing of hundreds of flies gathering to feed on the deads' blood, and the vultures circling in the clear blue sky.

2

At the same time the Trent gang was holding up the stagecoach, one hundred and seventy five miles to the north, Texas Rangers Will Kirkpatrick and Jonas Peterson were battling for their own lives. Right now the cards were stacked against them. For three days they had been trailing four men who'd held up the Quitaque State Bank, cleaning it out of every last penny, killing the bank's vice-president, a teller, and two customers in the process. They'd also shot down the town marshal as they made good their escape.

Will and Jonas had tracked the men into a thirty-four-mile long canyon at the edge of the *Llano Estacado* known as Blanco Canyon, which had been carved over eons by the White River. The entire two hundred and some miles long Caprock escarpment, which separated the *Llano Estacado* from the lower lands to the south and east, was a particularly rugged region of deep canyons, twisting arroyos, and sharp-edged ridges. It was a perfect hideout for outlaws, who took full advantage of the treacherous terrain. Will and Jonas had followed their quarry into a side canyon called Crawfish Canyon, which had been named after Crawfish Creek, the little stream that had carved it. The trail led into another, even narrower side canyon, which turned out to be a box.

"Jonas, it seems as if we've got 'em trapped in here," Will had said. "There's only one way outta this box, the same way we came in, which means they can't get past us."

Now, he was regretting his words. The outlaws either knew of, or had found, a hidden passage. It also seemed they had been aware of the lawmen dogging their trail for quite some time. They had doubled back and gotten to higher ground, finding good cover on the beetling cliffs. Most likely they had led Will and Jonas into a trap. The Rangers rode right into it. They were now pinned down, caught in a cross-fire from the bushed-up renegades. Will had taken a bullet through the biceps of his left arm at the first blast of gunfire, knocking him out of his saddle. The wound didn't seem life-threatening; however, it was bloody and painful. It also limited his maneuverability. He'd managed to crawl into a nest of boulders at the base of a talus slope, where he'd pulled off the wild rag which hung around his neck. He knotted the silk cloth around the wound to staunch the flow of blood. The fabric's brilliant crimson matched almost exactly the color of the blood oozing from the holes in Will's arm, making it difficult for him to determine how heavily he was bleeding. Making his predicament even more precarious, Pete, his stocky black and white overo paint gelding, had followed his training and streaked for safety when Will got shot and the bullets kept flying. Will's rifle was still on his horse. Jonas' bay gelding, Rebel, had also run for cover. Both mounts were hiding in a mesquite *bosque*, safe from any bullets except a freak ricochet, but where they were also impossible for the Rangers to reach. Any attempt to get to their horses would end with their being cut down in a hail of lead. While Jonas had pulled his Winchester from its scabbard when he rolled off his horse, Will had only his .45 Colt Single Action Army Peacemaker, which had nowhere near the range of the rifles handled by the murderous gang members. Worse, he only had the cartridges in the loops on his gun belt for ammunition. His spare shells for both rifle and pistol were still in his saddlebags. They might as well have been on the moon.

Will shook his head. If he or Jonas didn't figure a way out of this pickle, and soon, his wound, the loss of his rifle and horse, the blood he was losing, wouldn't matter. None of it would. Not with several more bullets having torn through both him and his partner, ending their lives. Right now Will wouldn't bet a plugged nickel that he and Jonas would live to see the sunset.

At the moment, the gunfire had slackened. Possibly the gang had decided to try and wait out their pursuers. It would be easy enough for them to wait until they could try and slip past the Rangers under the cover of darkness. Or more likely slip up on them, kill them to eliminate any further pursuit, and make their escape, most probably into the Indian Territories or New Mexico, out of reach of Texas law. Playing the waiting game was all in the outlaws' favor. They could choose the time and method they preferred to end this standoff. The longer they waited, the more hungry, thirsty, and weary the Rangers would get. And tired, hungry, and thirsty men got careless.

Will was feeling the effects of loss of blood and the sun beating down on him. He had to fight to keep from losing consciousness. He jerked back when a bullet struck just to the left of him, ricocheting off a rock and whining away, to land spent in the sand. Another shot rang out. One of the gang members screamed when he took a bullet from Jonas's rifle in his chest. He dropped back behind the fallen redberry juniper log he'd been using for cover.

Jonas, who was about ten feet away from Will, looked over at him and grinned.

"Hey, pardner, I appreciate you showin' yourself like that so I could get the damn fool that tried for you, but I wouldn't try that twice. The next one might not miss. I can't afford to let you get yourself killed dead. Not until my probation is over. At least the odds are down to three to one. Unless that son of a bitch is playin' possum.

I doubt it, though. I'm certain I nailed him dead center."

Will gave Jonas a weak grin. Several more bullets crashed into the rocks sheltering Will, and the log protecting Jonas. Flying bits of rock and splinters of wood forced the lawmen back to the dirt.

When the gunfire again stopped for a moment, Jonas chanced a glance at Will, who now was lying face-down and not moving.

"Will. *Will!*"

There was no response.

"Aw, hell. Dammit, Will, answer me. I'm not gonna let you die without a fight. You hear me? Say somethin'. Move a hand or foot if you can't talk. Even just wiggle a finger. Only lemme know you're still with me."

Still nothing.

There was absolutely no cover between Jonas's position and Will's. Jonas made an attempt to reach Will anyway, but was driven back by the outlaws' blazing guns. Jonas spent about two minutes studying the terrain and assessing the situation, then made his decision.

"I'm not goin' down without a fight," he muttered, taking one last look at Will, who still lay motionless. "Will, if you can hear me, hang in there, pard. God willing, I'll be back shortly. At least I sure hope so. If not, I'll see you on the other side of the Great Divide."

3

Jonas spotted what appeared to be a crack in the canyon wall, although he couldn't be certain. To reach it, he would have to cover about twenty yards of open ground. He murmured a silent prayer, then took off running. He kept low as he zig-zagged toward the narrow opening, with bullets hitting all around him. Just before he reached the crevice, he dove to his belly, rolled over twice, and fired at one of the killers who had exposed himself to view, in the mistaken belief Jonas was attempting to run off in panic, and would be an easy target. Jonas put a bullet through the man's gut. The outlaw screamed, doubled over, and tumbled from his perch. He rolled down the canyon's steep slope, almost all the way to the road, before his body was stopped by a boulder. A trail of dust marked his descent. Jonas dashed the last few feet to the opening. It was wider than he'd hoped. He got inside, then stopped for a moment to catch his breath.

The crevice was a natural chimney, wide enough for Jonas to brace his hands and feet on the sides, and scramble to the top. With luck, that would bring him out above the level of the two surviving outlaws. With even more luck, he'd have a clear shot at both of them. There was only one problem. To make the climb, he would need both hands free. That meant leaving his rifle behind. He'd have to rely on his expertise with the Smith and Wesson .44 revolver he wore butt forward on his right hip for a left-handed cross draw, and hope he could hit his targets despite the six-gun's much shorter range.

Luck was still with him. The chimney opened onto a rough ledge, which was covered with enough shattered rock and stunted brush to afford him plenty of cover. The two remaining outlaws were still looking at the spot where Jonas had disappeared, waiting to see if he showed himself again, or perhaps figure out that one of their bullets had found him, and ended his life. Their backs were to him.

Jonas wasn't taking any chances. The men had already robbed and killed five men, probably also believed they had finished off Will. Facing the hang rope, they'd have no compunction about adding Jonas to their list of victims. He crawled forward as far as he dared, careful not to make any but the slightest sounds, to allow for his revolver's short range. He aimed at the nearer man's back, thumbed back the hammer and pulled the trigger. His bullet struck the man low in his back. He arched in pain, screamed, fell to his hands and knees, then rolled onto his side. He lay twitching in his death throes. His shocked partner spun, attempting to find the source of the shot. Jonas put two quick bullets into his stomach. The last outlaw jackknifed and fell atop his downed partner.

"That takes care of the whole damn bunch," Jonas muttered. "Now to get back down and check on Will. I hope to God he's still alive."

Jonas took a moment to punch the empties out of his gun's cylinder and reload. He hurried back down the chimney. In his haste, he got careless. About ten feet before reaching the bottom, he missed a foothold. He grabbed frantically for a projecting rock, managed to get a tentative hold on it. The soft limestone broke off in his hand. Jonas plummeted to the bottom and landed on his back. Pain shot through him. He passed out.

4

When Will regained consciousness, he was propped against a rock. The left sleeve of his shirt had been cut off. He could feel the pressure of a bandage around his arm, which throbbed with pain. He opened his eyes to see Jonas leaning over him.

"Hey, Will. I'm sure glad to see you're back with me," Jonas said, grinning. "Boy howdy, I wasn't certain you'd make it. You bled for quite a while. I had trouble stopping the flow of blood. It was spurting pretty good. The slug must've nicked an artery."

"What . . . what happened? Where's the renegades we were chasin'? Or should I say had us dead to rights? And what the hell happened to you?"

Jonas's shirt was torn in several places. He had a number of scrapes and bruises, and dried blood plastered down his blonde hair on the left side of his head.

"It's like this, pardner. While you were sleepin', I took care of those *hombres*. After that, I came back and patched you up, best as I could."

"All of 'em?"

"Yeah. Here, you'd better take a few sips of this. Then I'll give you the whole story."

Jonas uncapped his canteen and held it to Will's lips.

"Not too much now," he warned, when Will started to gulp down the tepid, but still refreshing, water. Jonas pulled the canteen away. He sat down alongside Will, and took a swallow for himself.

"We're gonna spend the night here, then start back for Quitaque in the morning. You're too weak to ride very far, and I'm pretty beat up and hurting from the tumble I took. We both need to see a doc, especially you. You've lost a lot of blood. A good night's rest'll do us both a lot of good."

"I won't argue with you," Will said. "So how'd you manage to round up that bunch? I'm guessin' they're all dead."

"They are," Jonas confirmed. "After you passed out, I laid low for a while. I knew I had to find a way to get at the three left without gettin' shot all to pieces. I spotted what looked like an opening in the canyon wall, so I made a dash for it. Just before I got there, I pulled my patented act like I was running away, fall down, roll over twice, and let 'em have it right smack in the belly shot. Works every time. Sure enough, one of them fell for it, so I put a bullet into his gut. Bought me the few seconds I needed to reach the opening."

"I've seen you pull that move before," Will said. "I'm still amazed you haven't taken a bullet in your *own* belly, instead of one of the men you're after, for tryin' that stunt. One of these days your luck is bound to run out."

"It hasn't yet. And there's lots of other ways it might before that."

"I suppose you're right," Will conceded. "So give me the rest of the yarn."

"I caught a big break. The opening turned out to be a natural chimney, narrow enough for me to monkey up to its top. It ended at a ledge with plenty of cover. The two *hombres* left were still lookin' down to where they'd last seen me, tryin' to figure out where I'd gone. Since they were facin' the gallows in any event, and would for certain have killed again, I wasn't takin' any chances with 'em. I nailed one in the back before they had an inkling I'd gotten above them. The son of a bitch never knew what hit him. The other man tried to turn and get me, but he wasn't fast enough. I put two bullets through his middle."

"Where are they now? And you still didn't tell me why you look like you were dragged for half a mile by a runaway horse."

"The buzzards are already chowin' down on the three still up in the rocks. There was no easy way to get to them, and I wasn't about to risk breakin' my neck trying. I pulled the one who slid down to the road outta the brush, and wrapped him up in a blanket. Tucked the body where the buzzards and coyotes can't get to it. We'll take him along when we pull out in the morning. I located their horses up the trail a bit yonder. They're picketed with ours now. The stolen money was still in the saddlebags. We caught up with the gang before they had a chance to spend any of it."

"Except they almost paid us off in lead."

"I reckon that's so," Jonas agreed. "Anyway, I had no way of knowin' whether you were still alive, or dead. So once I was certain those no-good bastards were finished, and on their way to Hell, I tried to get back to you fast as I could. Guess I hurried a little too much. I missed a step comin' back down, and the rock I latched onto let go under my weight. I fell to the bottom of the chimney. Knocked myself out. Damn lucky I didn't break my neck or bust my skull wide open when I hit bottom. Don't know how long I was out cold. Once I came to, I looked myself over real quick, then took care of you. I know this is a dumb question, but how're you feelin', pardner?"

"Like I've been shot, ya damn fool. How d'ya think I'm feelin'?"

"Better'n I expected, to be honest," Jonas said. "I for sure figured you were a goner."

"You ain't getting rid of me that easily. Unless you want to go to Huntsville."

"Why do you think I work so hard to keep you alive?" Jonas said, chuckling.

Will laughed himself. He gave Jonas a back-handed slap to his belly.

"The rock you grabbed couldn't hold you, huh? I told you you'd been puttin' on a little weight around the middle there, pardner."

He slapped Jonas's belly again.

"Yup, definitely soft. Your gut'll be hangin' over your gun belt before too long. You've been chowin' down way too much, whenever we're in a town. You'll be givin' your poor horse a swayback."

"Don't you worry about Rebel," Jonas snapped. "He can carry me just fine. And I ain't any softer around my middle than I ever was. But if you pop me in the belly one more time I'll . . ."

"You'll what, Jonas? C'mon, say it. But be careful. Think about five years behind bars."

"I'll be plumb tickled you're feeling good enough to start a scrap, that's what."

"Smart boy. Also, thanks for savin' my hide, again. You're making a habit of pullin' my bacon out of the fire."

"Speaking of bacon, I'm hungry," Jonas said. "You?"

"I could stand to put some grub down my gullet."

"Good. You just take it easy while I build a fire and cook us up a mess of bacon and beans."

"Just don't burn the coffee this time."

"I never do. Simply like it strong. You want a smoke before I get started?"

"That's not a bad idea."

Jonas took the makings form his vest pocket. He rolled two quirlies, stuck one in his mouth, the other in Will's. He fished out a lucifer, struck it to life on a rock, and lit both cigarettes. While Will rested, Jonas busied himself with making an early supper. Before the sun reached the western horizon, their meal was finished, and both men were rolled in their blankets, fast asleep.

5

Early in the afternoon three days later, Will and Jonas rode back into Quitaque, which was pronounced "kitty-kay," leading the bank robbers' four horses, one of which carried the blanket wrapped body of its rider, lying draped belly down over its saddle and lashed in place. Shouts of surprise arose when the first townspeople saw the Rangers return. Word spread quickly through the small town. A crowd gathered and followed the two young lawmen as they made their way to the Quitaque Marshal's Office. Will and Jonas ignored their shouted questions.

There was a dust and sweat covered buckskin gelding tied to the hitch rail in front of the office. The weary horse, which had plainly been ridden hard and not yet been cared for, stood hip-shot, his head hanging low. A man wearing a Briscoe County deputy sheriff's badge, who had been loosening the buckskin's cinches, stopped to watch Will and Jonas as they reined up in front of the building. The deputy looked as worn out as his horse. He had a splotch of dried blood on his right arm, which was held against his chest by a neckerchief turned into a makeshift sling. Since Will and Jonas had pinned their silver star in silver circle badges to their vests before riding into town, he recognized them instantly as Texas Rangers. He nodded to them.

"Seems as if you boys have been busy. Deputy Sheriff Robert Turbert."

"Just a tad," Will answered. "Looks like you've been a mite busy yourself there, Deputy. Texas Ranger Will Kirkpatrick, and my pardner, Jonas Peterson."

"It appears we've got some stories to exchange," Turbert said. "You mind if that waits a few minutes? I need to take care of ol' Maverick here, then head on over to the doc and get myself patched up."

"We're headed there too, soon as our horses are groomed and grained," Jonas said.

"Jonas, I told you I'm feeling a lot better, and don't need a doctor," Will protested.

"You, the *hombre* who nearly passed out and fell off his horse three times yesterday alone? The man I nearly had to tie in his saddle? *You're* tellin' *me* you don't need medical treatment?" Jonas retorted. "Well, let me tell you something, Will Kirkpatrick. You do need a doctor, and you'll see one whether you like it or not. I didn't nursemaid you for the last hundred and fifty miles just to have you die on me now because of your dang stubborn streak. You're white as a ghost, you're runnin' a fever, and you've been slurring your words for the last four hours. You're in bad shape, whether you want to admit it or not. And I need to have my own hurts looked after. We've also got to notify the doc about this dead *hombre* so he can produce a coroner's report."

"I have to agree with your partner, Ranger," Turbert said. "You look to be in rough shape."

"Two goldang mother hens," Will muttered.

Homer Dwyer, the president of the Quitaque State Bank, hurried up. He looked from the Rangers, to the four horses they led, and back. He jerked a thumb at the dead man.

"I see you caught up with those sons of bitches. Where's the other three?"

Dwyer was in his late sixties, but appeared about ten years younger. He was still slim, his dark hair as thick as when he was a teenager, showing no signs of gray. He wore a boiled, starched white shirt, black tie, and a well tailored suit, one of several which he'd had custom made in Dallas. A heavy gold watch chain was draped across his middle. His only concession to age was the thick spectacles which shielded his brown eyes. Unlike the majority of west Texans, his skin was pale, since he spent most of his time inside his bank, or at home with Eleanor, his wife. In fact, he had been home, having dinner with her, when the bank was robbed. Dwyer had a demanding attitude which rubbed Will the wrong way the first time they'd met, after the robbery of Dwyer's bank. It still irked his liver, as his mother used to say, now.

"You'll have to ask my pardner," Will answered.

Dwyer turned to Jonas.

"Well?"

Jonas shrugged.

"Feeding the buzzards, last I saw."

"You mean you shot them down."

"They'd already killed five people right here in this town including the marshal, gunned down Will, and were doin' their damndest to get me too. So yeah. It seemed like the thing to do at the time. It was pure luck they didn't kill both of us. And if Will doesn't get to the doc right quick, he still might die."

Dwyer's pale face turned beet red.

"Don't get insolent with me, young man. I'll have your job."

"I doubt it. It don't pay all that much. Nowhere near what a banker makes. And it's a lot harder work. You don't appear to be the kind of man who likes to get his hands dirty."

"I can vouch for that," Will broke in. "My father's a successful banker back in central Texas. He's provided very well for my family. You have anything else you wish to say, Mr. Dwyer? If not, let us finish our business so we can have our wounds treated and get some rest."

"Just one. Did you retrieve my money?" Dwyer snapped.

"You mean your depositors' funds, don't you?" Will answered. "We recovered whatever the renegades had in their saddlebags. It will have to be counted to confirm they didn't perhaps stash some, planning to return for it once things quieted down."

"Then let's get that done."

Will shook his head.

"Uh-uh. Not yet. First we've got to get this body unloaded, and see if anyone recognizes him. It's already started to decompose. Then me'n Jonas, and it appears Deputy Turbert, need medical treatment. Our horses have to be put up for the night, then we'll have to get some supper, and a full night's rest. We'll count the money first thing in the morning. Until then, it will be held in the marshal's safe."

"You can't do that," Dwyer spluttered.

"My authority from the state of Texas says I can, and I will. If it makes you feel better, you can watch the money be put in the safe. Hell, you can even stand by the horses and guard it while we're at the *medico*'s."

"Ranger, if it's all the same to you, I'd like to make a suggestion," Turbert said. "If you think you can hold on for a few more minutes, we can put the money in the safe right now. We're right here at the office."

"I reckon you're right," Will agreed. "I guess mebbe I am feeling a bit worse than I thought.

I should have realized that. Soon as we put the cash away, we'll head for the doc's."

Over Dwyer's objections, the money was deposited in the Quitaque marshal's safe. After that, the three lawmen went to see Doctor Robert Lynch. Lynch's office was attached to his large, whitewashed home. One of the townspeople had run ahead to let him know to expect three patients, so Lynch was already prepared when they arrived. He had nine children, and ordered his two oldest boys to take the dead man from his horse and put him in the shed, until he treated the injured men. After all, the man wasn't going anywhere, except into the ground. He wouldn't mind waiting for the autopsy and coroner's inquest. Lynch's wife Sarah, who also acted as his nurse and assistant, ushered the wounded men into the examining and surgical room.

Lynch was a no-nonsense physician, in his early sixties, with too many years of treating gunshot and knife wounds under his belt. He took a quick look at the three men, and knew that Will required immediate treatment. The Ranger's flesh was deathly pale, his breathing labored. His eyes were glassy, and he was sweating profusely.

"Ranger Kirkpatrick, I need you to remove your shirt, then lie on your back on the table," he ordered.

"Sure, Doc."

Will removed his bloodied shirt. Sarah Lynch took it from him and set it aside. Lynch removed the bandage Jonas had wrapped around Will's arm. He took a closer look at the wound, which was red, inflamed, swollen, and hot to the touch. Will jerked and yelped when Lynch pressed a fingertip into the flesh just above the bullet hole.

"Sarah, I'll need a bottle of carbolic acid," he said. "Also a scalpel, as well as cloths to soak up any blood. Those will need to be placed in a pan of carbolic. We'll hold off on the bandages and dressings until I determine how much cutting needs to be done. I may also need a bone saw, if I decide amputation is necessary. In addition to the instruments, have some chloroform and laudanum ready."

"Amputation?" Will echoed. Despite his efforts to stay calm, his voice shook a bit.

"It's quite possible I may have to remove your arm from just above the wound, between your shoulder and elbow, yes," Lynch said. "Putrefaction has already set in. Once I open the wound and drain it, I'll be able to determine the extent of dead tissue, and how far any gangrene present has spread. I'm hoping I find very little, if any. I wasn't able to palpate any cold areas on your skin, so that's a good sign. Cold skin means tissue has already died. I do need to work quickly. Once gangrene does set in, it can spread rapidly throughout the entire body, resulting in a painful, fast death."

"There's no point in putting this off then, Doc. Please, get to work."

"I'm ready to start now, Ranger. I recommend you allow me to anesthetize you with chloroform. Once I start working on the wound, it will be extremely painful. Of course, there is always a risk involved with any anesthetic."

Will shook his head.

"I can't allow that. I was put under with that chloroform stuff once before. It nearly killed me. Got too much of it. I'll just take a knotted cloth to bite down on, if the pain gets to be too much. Please."

"I understand," Lynch said. "I don't agree with you, but I'll respect your request. I would recommend a dose of laudanum to dull the pain. For a man your size, I would say two tablespoons. No more than that."

Will nodded.

"I'll go along with you there."

"Excellent. Sarah, would you kindly give Ranger Kirkpatrick the laudanum? Also place a cloth in his mouth once he's swallowed all the medication."

"Of course, Robert."

Lynch turned to Jonas and Turbert while Sarah prepared a cloth for Will to bite on, and medicated him with the laudanum.

"I'm going to ask you men to help hold Ranger Kirkpatrick down," he said. "Since there's no bullet in his arm, and the wound is not to his torso, working on him won't be quite as dangerous as if I were probing for a bullet in his chest or abdomen. However, it's still vital he be kept as still as possible. I'd like each of you to take a shoulder, and press down hard when it becomes necessary."

"You've got it, Doc," Jonas agreed. He positioned himself at Will's right shoulder. Turbert took the left. Lynch removed the cloth from Will's mouth so he could speak.

"Are you feeling the effects of the laudanum yet, Ranger?"

Will nodded his head.

"It's warmin' my belly up just fine. And I'm startin' to feel a bit sleepy."

A look of concern crossed Lynch's face, gone as quickly as it appeared.

"Let's hope that's only from the laudanum, not from any infection which might have gotten into your blood, and worked its way to your brain."

"Hell, it's just an arm wound. Not much more'n a scratch," Will protested.

"A scratch which hasn't been treated properly for far too long. I'm not casting any aspersions on your work, Ranger Peterson," Lynch reassured Jonas. "You did the best you could. You may just have saved your partner's life. If it weren't for your ministrations, he would have died long before reaching town."

He turned his attention back to Will.

"The knot in this cloth is large enough? You don't feel as if you might swallow it and choke?"

"Not at all," Will answered.

"Then I'm going to get started."

Lynch slid the cloth back between Will's teeth. He poured carbolic solution over Will's arm, then took the scalpel out of the pan, dousing the blade yet again.

"Hold him down," he ordered Jonas and Turbert. "I'm going to make the first incision."

Lynch made his initial cut into the bullet hole in the front of Will's arm. Greenish-yellow pus spurted out, along with some blood. Lynch opened the incision wider, then put the scalpel back into the carbolic filled pan.

"I'm going to squeeze your arm, Ranger, to force as much pus out of the wound as I possibly can. Your arm is badly infected. Would you like more laudanum before I continue?"

Will shook his head. Beads of sweat popped out on his forehead. Sarah Lynch stood by with a clean, damp cloth to wipe his brow as needed.

Lynch applied pressure to both sides of Will's arm. Thick, viscous pus oozed from both the entrance and exit wounds. A foul stench filled the room. Will bit down on the cloth so hard he nearly broke his teeth.

"I'm sorry, Ranger. I'm being as gentle as I can be," Lynch apologized. "However, I have to get every last bit of pus and infection out of your arm, or it will just spread again. Do you understand?"

Will nodded his understanding.

Lynch kept the pressure on Will's arm, forcing out fluids until the pus gradually changed to blood, then clear lymphatic fluid.

Lynch let go of Will's arm and straightened up. He took a deep breath. Sarah took a fresh cloth to wipe his brow. Will had mercifully passed out.

"I'm going to cut away any dead tissue, then run a carbolic soaked cloth through the wound to kill any remaining infection," he explained to Jonas and Turbert. "After that, I'll pour some more carbolic solution into the wound, and cover it loosely with a carbolic soaked bandage. I can't pack the wound and bandage it tightly right now. I need to let it drain first. I don't believe there's so much damage yet I'll have to amputate. You men got him here just in time. I may decide to cauterize the wound, if later I think that would be necessary to avoid amputation. All we can do once I finish with Ranger Kirkpatrick is let him rest, wait, and pray. I'd suggest you both go into the waiting room until I call for you."

"What if Will wakes up?" Jonas asked.

"He won't," Lunch assured him. "Frankly, I'm

amazed he remained conscious as long as he did, between the loss of blood and the infection. With the laudanum I gave him, he finally quit fighting to stay awake. Several hours' rest is the best medicine for him now. I'm hoping he sleeps through the night."

"Let's go, Ranger," Turbert said. "We can have a smoke while we're waiting. I could use one. I'd wager you could too."

"No smoking inside," Turbert said. "I won't even smoke my pipe in the office or house. You can go onto the front porch. There are benches out there if you want to sit down."

"That sounds good," Jonas answered. "Let's go, Deputy."

Jonas and Turbert sat down in a swing on the front porch. They took out sacks of Bull Durham, cigarette papers, and matches from their vest pockets. They each rolled and lit quirlies.

Jonas leaned back and took a long drag on his cigarette, then exhaled a ring of smoke from between his lips.

"So what brought you to Quitaque, Deputy, and how'd you get yourself shot?" he asked.

"We might as well call each other by our first names, long as it's all right with you," Turbert said. "I go by Bob."

"It's fine with me. I stick with Jonas. You gonna answer my question?"

"Yup. After the bank robbery, when you and your pardner took off on the trail of the perpetrators, the town sent a message to Silverton asking the county sheriff to send down a deputy to cover the place until a new marshal could be hired, or at least until you and your pardner returned. I was the only man available, so I was given the job. It's not all that far from the county seat at Silverton to here, so I arrived the next day."

"How'd you get shot?"

"I'm comin' to that. The first couple of days were peaceful and quiet. Then Saturday night rolled around. And it was payday. As usual, a bunch of ranch hands from the surrounding outfits rode into town to blow off some steam and spend their money on whiskey, gambling, and women. There were the usual few who got out of hand, but the threat of a night behind bars cooled 'em off pretty quick. However, there was one, Justin Frank . . ."

"That name sounds familiar," Jonas broke in.

"It should. His family owns the Circle F Ranch. It's the biggest cattle operation in this part of the Panhandle. Covers more than half of Briscoe County and a good piece of Hall County. Justin's the youngest boy. He's always been trouble, ever since he was a tadpole. A real hothead. He can't do any wrong in the eyes of his Ma and Pa. His sisters and older brothers, too. They all spoiled him rotten. Anyway, Justin got into an argument with Randy Hollis, the head wrangler at the KR Ranch, over one of the gals at Miss Dolly's Social Club. It started with words, then escalated to fists. Randy beat the stuffings out of Justin. That hurt Justin's pride, I guess. He couldn't leave things be. So he pulled out his gun and shot Randy . . . in the back. Four times. One of his bullets went clean through Hollis and killed Bessie Sparks, the woman they'd been fightin' over. But Justin wasn't finished. He was still in a rage. He reloaded his pistol and put six more bullets into Hollis's back, while he was already lying dead on the floor. Once his mad wore off, he must've known that even his family couldn't protect him from a cold-blooded, back-shootin' murder, plus killing an innocent woman. But he also realized they were the only chance he had. So he and the rest of the Circle F boys lit a shuck for home. I went after them, but they reached the ranch before I caught up with 'em. The Franks were waitin' for me. I only got the chance to fire two shots before one of 'em, don't know which one, put a slug into my arm. I reckon it was meant for my chest. I knew I didn't have a chance against the entire outfit, so I headed back here until I could round up some reinforcements. It's a two day ride between Quitaque and the Frank ranch. I reached town just before you fellers. I was gonna send for a couple more deputies to come down from Silverton, but I had to get patched up first."

"Maybe we can recruit some men from town," Jonas suggested.

Bob shook his head.

"Not a chance. The merchants know who butters their bread. The rest of the town is too buffaloed by the Franks to stand up to them."

"Then I reckon it's up to me'n you," Jonas said. "We can't give Justin time to make a getaway, if he hasn't already. Soon as the doc treats our wounds, we'll hit the trail again."

"What about horses? My Msverick's plumb worn out, and your cayuse didn't look in such great shape, neither."

"Some oats and hay in his belly and two hours' rest, and Rebel will be ready to go again. If your bronc isn't, we'll rent one at the livery stable. But we can't let that kid get away with murder."

Bob sighed.

"You're right. Maverick'll do what I ask of him."

"Then it's settled. Soon as we're fixed up, we go arrest Justin Frank," Jonas said.

"You haven't told me what happened to you and your pardner," Bob reminded him. "Although I gather no one has to worry about the sons of bitches who raided the Quitaque bank. Not anymore."

"No, they don't," Jonas said. "Me'n Will

tracked them into Blanco Canyon, then up Crawfish Canyon. But they'd fooled us. Led us into a trap. Shot Will outta the saddle, and had us both pinned down. One of them made a mistake. He showed himself when he tried to put another bullet into Will. I drilled him dead center. But we were still pinned down, and still outnumbered three to two, plus they had the high ground. Then Will passed out. I was determined if I was gonna go down, I was goin' down fightin'. I spotted a crack in the canyon wall and made a run for it. Fooled one of the outlaws into thinkin' I was tryin' to make a break for it. I let him have it right in his gut. When I reached the crack, it turned out to be a natural chimney that went all the way to the top of the wall. I climbed it, and it brought me out above the two men who were left. I gunned them both down before they had a chance to get me. Left those two, and their pardner, up in the rocks. The first one I'd plugged fell to the road. He's the one we brought back."

"But it looks like they did get you," Bob said.

"Nah, I did this to myself," Jonas explained. "I was in too much of a hurry comin' back down, tryin' to get to Will. Missed a foothold. I grabbed a protruding rock to try'n stop my fall, but it gave way. I scraped myself up pretty good, and knocked myself out when I hit bottom. Once I came to, I patched up Will best I could, then we spent the night right there, and started back first thing the next morning."

The door opened. Sarah Lynch came onto the porch.

"The doctor is ready to see you now," she said.

Jonas and Bob stubbed out their quirlies, tossed the butts into the dirt, and followed her inside.

6

After being treated for their injuries, Jonas and Bob would pass the night resting. They planned on leaving for the Circle F Ranch shortly after sunup. Before they turned in for the night, they did stop by Dr. Lynch's office on their way to bed, to check and see how Will was doing. Lynch informed them Will's fever had worsened over the past several hours, and he had slipped into a coma. Lynch would try and help Will's body fight off the infection by keeping him as cool as possible with the use of cold, wet cloths and damp sheets, and keeping him sedated.

Jonas and Bob spent the night sleeping in the cells at the marshal's office. An hour before sunrise, just as the first gray light of the false dawn was streaking the eastern sky, they were jolted out of their sleep by the pounding hoof beats of a dozen hard-ridden horses, and the shouts and curses of their riders. They barely had time to throw off their blankets and grab the pistols lying next to their bunks before the riders stopped in front of the office. They had to dive on their bellies to the floor as a barrage of bullets raked the building, shattering the windows and punching through the walls. Several of the slugs ricocheted wildly around the room, after striking the potbellied stove or a cell bar. One punched through the coffee pot and sent it flying, splashing its remaining contents everywhere.

"What the hell?" Jonas yelled.

"Deputy! Deputy Turbert! This is Stanley Frank. You killed my boy. Now we're gonna kill you. You gonna come out and take it like a man, or are we gonna have to burn you out like the snivelin' coward you are?"

"I didn't kill your boy, Frank," Bob answered. "I barely had a chance to get off a couple of shots before one of your men drilled me. I'm just lucky whoever got me is a bad shot. So was I for that matter, at least last night. I didn't even hit a window, let alone Justin."

"Don't try'n lie to me, Deputy. You plugged Justin right in his belly. He took almost two days to die, gut-shot, in terrible agony. He never said a word after he got it, just cried and moaned from the pain. His ma and sisters tried to help him, but all they could do was watch him die. We're here to avenge his death by doin' the same to you."

"Lemme try'n talk some sense into those *hombres*," Jonas said. He raised his voice.

"Mr. Frank. This is Texas Ranger Jonas Peterson. I don't know if this here deputy killed your son or not, if he is indeed dead, and you're not tryin' to hide him. But whatever happened, your boy brought it on himself. I had a chance to talk with Doctor Lynch. He confirmed the man your son killed was shot ten times in the back. Justin had to be brought in to face two charges of murder, for the man he killed, and the woman. If the deputy didn't bring him in, then me or my pardner would have. I understand there are plenty of witnesses to the killing. I'll be questioning them as soon as possible."

"He was defendin' himself. That son of a bitch Hollis beat him half to death for no reason."

"That's for a court to decide, not you. The Rangers don't tolerate vigilante mobs. If you want to press charges against Deputy Turbert, that's your right. But if you kill him, I'll have to place you and everyone else involved under arrest."

"I've got no beef with you, Ranger. It's with that murderin' deputy. Turn him over to us, and you can ride out of Quitaque a free man. Fight us, and you'll die along with Turbert."

"I'm not about to turn any man over to a lynch mob. And if I do die here this mornin', I'll take some of you with me," Jonas said. "You'll be the first one to take a slug, Frank. I promise you that. And once my pardner's up and around again, he'll track down the rest of you. A Ranger don't quit the trail of anyone who kills another Ranger. Not ever."

"I'll give you ten minutes to change your mind, Ranger," Franks answered. "If Turbert doesn't come out when the time's up, we'll be comin' in after him. There's twelve of us and only two of you. Six to one odds. That's not any bet a smart gamblin' man would take."

"Call me a fool gambler, then, because I like those odds," Jonas answered.

"You just signed your own death warrant, Ranger. Ten minutes."

Jonas looked around the office.

"You think we have a chance of reachin' those shotguns and rifles in the rack without gettin' ourselves shot to ribbons, Bob?"

"I reckon, if we're quiet about it. The shades are still down, although they are full of bullet holes, so the men outside probably can't see us. We'd better make our move *pronto*, though. Daylight's not all that far off."

"You think anyone in town might take a hand?"

"On our side? No. Probably not Frank's, either. I'll bet not a lamp was lit. Folks'll stay hidden indoors, nice and safe, until this thing is settled, one way or the other."

"They usually do," Jonas said. "You stay put. I'll get us each a rifle and shotgun."

Jonas pulled himself by his elbows across the rough wood plank floor. He gave a soft yelp.

"You all right, Jonas?" Bob whispered.

"Yeah, I reckon. Just got a splinter in my ribs. It's nothing. I've already pulled it out. Sure wish we'd had time to grab our shirts and boots."

He reached the gun rack, got up, snatched down two rifles and two shotguns, then belly crawled his way back to Turbert. He handed the deputy a rifle and shotgun.

They could hear the men outside dismounting and taking up positions around the office. The horses were being led away, out of the range of any stray bullets.

"One or two of 'em'll probably go around back," Bob said. "I'll close the door to the cells. It's solid oak, so it'll stop most bullets."

"It won't stop the flames if they throw a torch or two on the roof or through the cell windows," Jonas said.

"Damn, Ranger. You sure are a cheerful cuss."

"I'll be a lot more cheerful once we get outta this fix."

After turning over a desk and jamming it against the door, Jonas stationed himself at the left front window, Bob the right. Sunrise was fast approaching. The men from the Circle F Ranch, who moments before had been shadowy figures in the dim pre-dawn light, could now be seen more clearly. Minutes ticked by while they settled into their chosen spots. Jonas and Bob each braced a shotgun on their respective windowsills, and thumbed back the hammers on both barrels. Sweat trickled down their backs and chests. It beaded on their foreheads and dampened their hair.

Stanley Frank's call broke the silence.

"Time's up. You comin' out Deputy, or do we have to come in there and drag you out?"

"You can try, and you'll probably succeed, but you'll pay an awful high price," Bob answered.

"I'll take that chance."

Frank gave an order to one of his men. A torch was lit, and under a covering volley of gunfire, the man carrying it ran for the office, intending to throw the torch onto the wooden roof and set the building aflame.

Jonas squeezed one of the triggers on his shotgun. The spreading buckshot ripped through the torch bearer's right arm. It peppered his right shoulder, his upper right chest, his face, and tore open his throat. With a stifled scream, he dropped the torch, staggered and fell atop it, snuffing out the flame. The acrid odors of burnt cloth and flesh filled the air.

The gunfire stopped momentarily.

"They got Grody, damn them," Frank shouted. "Let 'em have it! Pour it into 'em."

Jonas and Bob hugged the floor as another barrage of lead tore into the front of the building. Two shots rang out from another direction. Two more of Frank's men yelled when bullets knocked them to the ground. One of them was Barney Frank, the oldest son.

"Stop!" someone ordered. "Stop shootin'."

The gunfire abated.

"Why'd you tell us to stop shootin', Chad?" Frank asked the second youngest of his four sons. "We had those sons of bitches pinned down."

"Because someone else just took a hand, and now we're caught in a crossfire. Whoever it is got Barney and Jack Poole. They're both dead, seems like. Enough of this is enough, unless you want to see us wiped out. The deputy didn't kill Justin. I did."

"What're you sayin', boy?"

"I said, the deputy didn't kill Justin. I did."

"You? But why? How?"

"Because Justin had finally gone too far, backshootin' a man and killin' a woman. This entire family let him get away with doin' whatever he wanted for far too long. Ever since he was a baby. He was gonna cost you everything you and Ma worked for, Pa. I'm as much to blame as the rest of the family. We all mollycoddled him. When Justin showed up at the house, with the deputy on his tail, and said what he'd done, I knew he had to be stopped once and for all. When the gunfight at home started, I left the front of the house and went back to where Justin was hidin'. I tried to sneak up on him, and knock him out with my gun barrel over his head, but he heard me comin'. He took a shot at me but missed. So I shot him. I didn't want to. I wanted to turn him over to the law. I had no choice, Pa. If I hadn't killed Justin, he'd have killed me. He didn't care about anyone but himself. I woke up to that too late. I guess I'm the only one who did."

"Why didn't you tell me this before?"

"Because I was a coward. Like this whole family is a bunch of cowards. All of us were too afraid of Justin to stop him. I'm just sorry I didn't do somethin' about him sooner."

"I'm sorry too, Chad. Sorry that you killed your baby brother."

Franks turned his gun on Chad, and fired one shot. The bullet hit Chad in his stomach. Chad grunted, placed a hand over the bullet hole, but still stood tall as blood oozed between his fingers.

"Why . . . why'd you do . . . that, Pa? Why'd you shoot . . . me, your own . . . son?"

"Because I don't abide traitors, and you're a traitor to your family, boy. You know the only real law around here is Frank law."

"Then I guess . . . I'd better . . . fix that. I love . . . you, Pa. Sorry."

Chad thumbed back the hammer of his .44 Remington, and pulled the trigger. He shot his father through the bridge of his nose, putting a bullet deep into his brain. Father and son fell. They hit the ground at the same time. Stunned silence followed.

"It's over. The rest of you, drop your guns. Unless you also want to end up dead."

"That's Will!" Jonas exclaimed. "He ain't supposed to be out of bed. We'd better get out there and lend him a hand."

He and Bob hurried outside. Will was leaning against the side of the millinery shop, using the building for support. But the shotgun he held was unwavering. The surviving members of the raiding party had obeyed his order, and dropped their weapons to the dirt.

"All of you, stand in the middle of the street. Side by side," Will ordered. "You've got three guns on you, so I'd advise you don't so much as twitch."

"You mind if I check on my brother?" Colby Frank, the sole surviving son, asked.

"Go ahead, but no false moves," Will said. "The rest of you, do what I said."

"We've got the others covered, Will," Jonas said. "You take it easy."

"I'll go with that boy while he checks on his brother."

Will walked just behind Colby. They walked up to Chad, who was lying face down. Blood flowed freely from the exit wound in his back.

"Go ahead, roll him over," Will told Colby.

Colby knelt alongside his dying brother. He rolled him gently onto his back.

"Chad."

"Colby. Reckon you're . . . the head of the family . . . now. Hope . . . you're up to the . . . job. I'm sorry for havin' to kill . . . to kill . . ."

"Shh. I know."

"Tell Ma, and my sisters . . . I . . . love them."

"I'll do that."

"Good."

Chad led out a long sigh. He went slack.

Will nudged Colby's shoulder.

"Your brother's gone. We'd better get back to the others, so we can straighten things out, as much as we can."

They went back to where the seven surviving Circle F men stood, their hands in the air as they were guarded by Jonas and Bob. Now that the gunfire was over, a crowd was beginning to gather. People were emerging from their houses, gathering in morbid curiosity. Little boys in particular stared wide-eyed at the corpses. Before the day was out, they would be reenacting the gunfight on the streets and in their yards. Their bodies would be scattered on the ground. To the young, death, even after seeing its reality, was still an abstract concept. You got shot, fell down dead, then in a minute or two got back up and generally shot the friend who had shot you. Then the game started all over again. There was no finality to death when it was just a game. Sadly, none of those boys realized some of them would also be lying dead from a bullet, before being out of their teens.

"You men, listen carefully, as I'm only gonna say this once," Will said. "There's been enough dyin' here today, As far as I'm concerned, and I'll make certain Sheriff Harvester goes along, this matter is finished, It's a tragedy for everyone involved. There's no point in putting any of you in jail. You've all been punished enough by what happened here today. You'll all be charged with breach of peace, and I'll have the judge sentence you to a fine and probation. Restitution for damages to the marshal's office will have to be made, but once the dust settles, I'm certain the Circle F will take care of that. Colby Frank, since you are the only surviving representative of the ranch here today, will you agree to those conditions?"

"I will. I just want to get my pa and brothers home for a decent burial."

"Doc Lynch will have to sign the death certificates, then you can be on your way. I see him comin' now."

Lynch walked up to Will.

"Ranger, I should have known I'd find you here. You're a damn fool, I hope you know that. I didn't even realize you'd regained consciousness until I heard all the gunfire, came into your room to get my medical bag, and found you gone."

"You ain't the first one to call me that, and you won't be the last," Will said. "There's three men here you'll have to pronounce deceased. I don't believe there's any wounded who need treatment."

"What about your partner?"

"I'm not hurt," Jonas said.

"Are you certain about that?" Lynch asked.

Will looked at Jonas and started laughing.

"You'd better take a look at your gut, pardner. Any Comanche, Kiowa, or Apache would be proud of makin' that shot with a bow and arrow. Someone got you clean in your belly button."

Jonas looked down at his middle, gagged, and became nauseous. Sure enough, one of the splinters which had been shot off the office wall by a bullet was protruding from his belly button. A small trickle of blood ran from it down Jonas's lower abdomen and disappeared behind his denims' waistband. There was no way of knowing how deeply the splinter had buried itself in his guts. It was quite possible it had perforated an intestine.

"You mean you didn't realize you had that thing sticking out of you?" Bob asked.

"Nope, I didn't. Reckon in all the excitement I didn't feel it hit me. But now that I know it's there, it hurts like hell."

"Get right down to my office and I'll remove it," Lynch said. "Don't attempt to pull it out yourself. It's helping slow the flow of blood. In addition if the splinter did perforate an intestine, removing it haphazardly could lead to bowel material leaking into the abdominal cavity. That would lead to an infection, peritonitis, and death.

Wrap a cloth around it and hold it in place until I can remove it. Ranger Kirkpatrick, you need to return immediately also. I have to make certain you haven't undone all my work in repairing your arm. You also still have a serious infection."

"You both listen to the doctor's orders," Bob said. "I'll take charge of things here if you'll just take a few minutes to confirm the deaths, Doc."

"I'll do that. The official certificates can wait."

"*Gracias.* That's good, because the surviving son wants to take the bodies home. He's still in shock, and exhausted."

"You two Rangers go on ahead," Lynch ordered. "I'll be along in a few minutes. Ranger Kirkpatrick, you get right back in bed. Ranger Peterson, I still don't want you to attempt to remove that splinter on your own. It may be a simple procedure, or, if it has perforated a gut, removal could be quite complicated, as I will need to repair the gut and make certain no infection sets in. Your wound can wait the few minutes it will take me to care for your partner."

"All right. Will, let's go, before you fall flat on your face. I'll grab my boots and shirt on the way."

7

Doctor Lynch arrived back at his office about thirty minutes after Will and Jonas. Will was still conscious, but his face was flushed, and he was perspiring profusely. Sweat rolled down his chest and back.

"I was hoping you'd fall back to sleep before I got here, Ranger," Lynch said.

"I had to remain awake until I see whether that splinter turned Jonas's belly button from one stickin' out to one pressing in," Will joked. He managed a short chuckle.

"Your partner's belly button is the least of your worries. If the infection you have turns into blood poisoning, it will go through your entire system. You'll be dead in less than a week, probably no more than two or three days. And you'll suffer horribly before you die. I'm going to clean and disinfect your arm again, before I work on Ranger Peterson."

"I won't argue with you," Will said. "Do you mind if me'n Jonas talk while you work on us?"

"Not at all, if you'll wait until after I finish with you. Then, go right ahead. However, you need more sleep, so I will be giving you another dose of laudanum. You should have sufficient time to hold your discussion before you fall asleep."

"I'd rather have a bottle of good Kentucky bourbon."

"So would I, Ranger. So would I."

Lynch unwrapped the old bandage from around Will's arm and tossed it into a trash can. He cleaned the wound with soap and water, and doused his hands, then the wound, with carbolic solution.

"I'm going to try and force more pus out of the wound. Are you ready, Ranger?"

Will nodded.

Lynch pressed down hard on the wound, expelling pus from both the entrance and exit holes. The pus was soon replaced by blood, then clear fluids.

"You're healing more quickly than I anticipated. There's nowhere near the volume of pus that I expected," Lynch said. "However, you're going to have to remain here and endure bed rest for at least the next two weeks. The wound has to drain for several more days, then it will need to be sutured. I can't discharge you until I'm certain all traces of infection are gone."

"I could just get up and leave," Will said.

"You could, but I wouldn't advise that. There's no possible way for your wound to be kept as sterile as possible except by being confined here. Dirt would be certain to work its way behind the bandage and into the wound, causing a new infection. You'd be worse off than you are now.

The odds of your surviving a second infection are next to nothing."

"Listen to the doc, Will," Jonas urged. "You've had a rough few days. The bad guys will still be waiting for us once you're up and around."

"I reckon," Will said, clearly not convinced. "You'll just need to work without me for a while. You'll have to return to our post at Sweetwater. Keep a lid on things the best you can, until I'm fit to ride again. I'll send you a telegram when I'm on my way. Make sure to keep me posted on what you're up to."

Jonas shook his head.

"That won't work, Will. I'm still on probation, and in your custody."

Jonas had been forced to take part in a stagecoach robbery by his two cousins. Will tracked them down. When he caught up with them one of the cousins resisted arrest, attempted to gun Will down, and died for his effort. The other cousin and Jonas surrendered. However, when preparing to leave for Pecos the next day, that man tricked Will, disarmed him, and was about to kill him. Jonas intervened, and in the ensuing fight ended up killing his kin, thus saving Will's life.

Since Jonas was still guilty of taking part in the robbery, he remained Will's prisoner. At Jonas's trial in Pecos, Will related the circumstances of how Jonas had been an unwilling participant, and how he had saved the Ranger's life. The presiding judge took mercy on Jonas. He sentenced him to five years in the state prison at Huntsville. However, the sentence was suspended on the condition Jonas would be on probation, would be in Will's custody for the duration, and would need to become a Texas Ranger. He'd been riding with Will ever since.

"It will have to," Will answered. "Before you leave, I'll write up a letter explaining the situation, as well as send a telegram to the court back in Pecos, so they don't think you're tryin' to pull a fast one. Bad enough to have one of us out of commission. Having both of us out of action just isn't acceptable. The renegades will ride roughshod over this entire territory."

"Ranger Kirkpatrick, please hold still so I can finish bandaging your arm," Lynch said.

"Sure."

Will forced himself to relax while the doctor worked on him. Just as Lynch was finished, a knock came on the door. Sarah Lynch walked into the room, followed by a scrawny, pimple-faced, tow-haired teenager.

"I'm sorry to interrupt, Robert, but Theodore just received a telegram for the Rangers," Sarah said. "He says it's important, and can't wait."

"It's all right, Sarah. Come in, Teddy."

"Thanks, Doc."

"I'll take the message," Will said. "Jonas, do

you have a nickel you can give the boy? I ain't exactly in a position where I can reach into my pockets easily."

"Sure, Will."

Jonas dug a nickel out of his pants pocket and handed it to the young telegrapher, who in turn handed the yellow flimsy bearing the message to Will.

"I apologize for the delay on behalf of Western Union, Rangers," Teddy said. "The wires were down between here and Sweetwater for several days. Might've been a thunderstorm, might've been some longhorn or other critter knocked down a pole while usin' it to scratch its back. Hell, it even could've been a bird landing on the wrong piece of wire, or some rodent chewin' through 'em. Any of a hundred things. The repairs were just completed. This message was the first to come in. I could tell it was important, so I brung it right over."

"Don't worry about that. You have no control over what Mother Nature might do," Will assured him.

"I'd better get back to the office. There'll be a passel more messages coming in. And I've got a whole pile to send out."

"You go ahead, son. *Muchas gracias* for hurrying over here," Will said. "We're obliged."

When Will read the message, his expression grew grim.

"What's it say?" Jonas asked. "From the look on your face it can't be good news."

"It damn sure isn't. There's been three stagecoach robberies between Abilene and Sweetwater in the past two weeks. No witnesses left alive at any of 'em. The outfit hits fast, kills the driver, guard, and passengers, grabs what they want, and gits. No one has even seen a sign of them. The only odd thing is the gang does leave the horses behind and still hitched, which is kind of unusual."

"They must have a conscience. They want to make it easier to bring the dead into town," Jonas said.

"Yeah, right." Will shook his head. "I reckon you'd better start back for Sweetwater this afternoon. Send the telegram to Pecos and mail the letter to Austin before you leave here. It won't take me long to write them up."

"I'll push Rebel as hard as I can. Mebbe I'll come across that murderin' bunch."

"Don't get any damn fool ideas about takin' on a gang like that all on your lonesome, Jonas," Will warned. "That'd be too hard a job for a veteran Ranger to tackle singlehandedly, let alone one who's still learning the ropes."

"Are you saying you don't want me to return to Sweetwater, Will?"

"Not at all. Find out everything you can about the outfit, which doesn't sound like it'll be much, then deputize some good men to help you. Recruit some from the Nolan County Sheriff. Then once you get a good lead as to where those *hombres* might be, go after them. You'll also have other renegades you'll run across, too. Do the best you can, but don't get in over your head. Keep me and Austin posted. I'll be out of this bed and on my way to catch up with you soon as I can."

"All right. I'll be ridin'. You take it easy, Will."

"You seem to be forgetting something, Ranger Peterson. I've still got to remove the splinter from your navel," Lynch said.

"From my what?"

"Your navel. Your belly button."

"Oh. Why didn't you say that? For a minute I thought you were talking about a boat, Doc."

"Different spelling, Ranger. N-a-v-e-l is the belly button. N-a-v-a-l refers to a vessel, usually part of a military fleet."

"I know that, Doc. Just makin' a joke. I was figuring on pulling that splinter out myself. It's not much bigger than a sliver."

"You might want to remember I'm about to put a scalpel into your gut before telling any more jokes that bad," Lynch scolded. "You also let me be the judge of how serious your wound is. There's no way of telling how deeply the splinter penetrated until it's pulled out. Just the quick look I had earlier seemed to indicate it may have gone deeply enough to tear a hole in an intestine.

It may also have splintered into a number of pieces beneath the skin. Either scenario increases the likelihood of an infection forming. It's vital I make certain there's no leakage of bowel material, and all pieces of wood have been found and removed. Caring for you should only take a few minutes, unless there are complications. So please, lie down on the table and open your shirt."

"You ain't givin' me a choice, Doc, are you?"

"No, I'm not. Of course, you could refuse. But if you develop peritonitis it will spread into your abdominal cavity and organs such as the liver, spleen, or kidneys. It would also enter your bloodstream and give you blood poisoning. You'll die almost exactly as if you were gut-shot. Painfully, and slowly. So yes, you do have a choice."

"Not when you put it like that," Jonas said. He climbed onto the table, stretched out on his back, unbuttoned and opened his shirt.

"I'm ready."

"This is going to sting," Lynch warned.

Jonas winced when the doctor poured carbolic into his belly button and over the surrounding area.

"Are you still all right?" Lynch asked. "You're not feeling sick to your stomach, or like you might have to throw up? Any sharp or extreme belly pain?"

Jonas shook his head.

"Not at all."

"That's good, If you were, it could indicate the splinter had perforated an intestine. Carbolic leaking into the gut would provoke such a reaction. I'm about to go ahead and remove the splinter."

Lynch took a small forceps, clamped it around the splinter, and pulled it out. Blood began flowing more freely from the wound. He set the forceps aside and picked up a pair of tweezers.

"Sarah, would you please wipe away the blood, so I can look for any other slivers?"

"Of course, Robert."

Sarah soaked a cloth with carbolic, then soaked it in cold water. She used that to wipe away blood while her husband probed for any more slivers. He removed three, then straightened up. He arched his back to remove a kink.

"I believe I got all the slivers out, and there's no sign your intestine was perforated, Ranger. I'm going to use a styptic pencil to stop the bleeding. Once the flow has stopped, I'll place a loose bandage over your wound, and tie it in place. There's no practical way to sew up the wound, but I will attempt it if you'd prefer."

"Suture self," Jonas said.

"Wow. There's a real knee slapper I haven't already heard a hundred times or more," Lynch replied, shaking his head. He jabbed the styptic pencil into Jonas harder than he'd intended. "You'll have me in stitches."

"Ow. Take it easy, Doc."

"Sorry. But I did warn you about making any more bad jokes."

"Will I still be able to leave for Sweetwater today?"

"I don't see any reason why not. The wound still needs to drain, so you'll have to change the bandage regularly to keep it clean. I can give you a sufficient supply until you reach your destination. Once you do, have a physician there examine the wound again. Do you carry a shaving kit in your saddlebags? Does it contain a styptic pencil?"

"I do, and it does," Jonas answered.

"Good. If the wound starts bleeding excessively again, use that to stem the flow. I'm not talking about a small amount, which is to be expected. However, if blood starts flowing out of your navel and down your lower abdomen, you'll need to use the styptic. Smoking tobacco can also be used in a pinch. It also helps prevent infection. Make certain you keep the wound as dry as possible. The belly button is naturally damp with sweat, and dark inside, so any injuries to it are prone to infection. Most importantly, if you develop any redness or swelling around the wound, see a red line going up a blood vessel from it, start running a fever, or have sharp belly pain, get to the nearest doctor as quickly as possible."

"That might be easier said than done. There's not much in the way of settlements between here and Sweetwater. A couple of small villages, and an occasional ranch or farmhouse, but that's all."

"Then you'll have to be extra cautious you don't tear open your wound more than it is. I truly wish I could take a few stitches in it, but that's not possible."

"We also carry wound powder for our horses," Will broke in. "Jonas can use that. Since his horse is smarter than he is, it might also help his brain."

"Both our horses have more sense than we do," Jonas shot back.

"I can't argue with that, and I've only just met the two of you," Lynch said. "Once I finish up you can be on your way, Ranger Peterson."

"Not quite," Will said. "Since I'm still laid up, he'll have to send the telegram off to the court in Pecos, and the letter to Ranger Headquarters. If you have a pencil and paper I can use, Doc, I'll write those up. *Then* Jonas can head on out."

"I'll get them for you," Sarah said.

"*Gracias.* I'm obliged."

The letter and telegraph message were written.

"You be careful," Will told Jonas, who took and tucked the papers into his vest pocket.

"I will be. You just take it easy so you heal up quick," Jonas answered. "*Adios*, pard. I'll see you in Sweetwater."

"*Vaya con Dios*, Jonas."

8

It was approximately one hundred and sixty miles from Quitaque to Sweetwater. Steadily riding at a normal pace a man on horseback could cover the distance in five days. Pushing hard, it could be done in three. Jonas intended to split the difference, and make the journey in four. By doing so, he wouldn't overtax himself or his horse.

The day, already hot, became more humid as Jonas headed south.

"It'll cool off once the sun goes down, Rebel," he told his horse, patting the gelding's sweat soaked neck. "We'll have to travel for a few hours in the dark. Good thing the moon's almost full. There's no drinkable water until we reach Roaring Springs, so it's gonna be a while. Once we get there, and you cool off, you can have a long, cold drink, and all the grass your belly can hold. Mebbe we'll sleep in a little come morning."

Rebel snorted. He shook his head.

"No, I'm not tryin' to pull a fast one on you, horse," Jonas said, laughing. "We'll get a good rest before we start out again."

Jonas reached Roaring Springs just around nine-thirty that night. The waterhole had once been the site of a Comanche encampment. It was the only dependable source of cool, pure, sweet water for miles in any direction. Jonas was the only traveler there tonight, which was a bit unusual. Due to its dependable water source, Roaring Springs was a popular overnight stopping place.

Jonas rode over to the spring. Rebel lowered his muzzle into the water. The parched mustang pawed at the water, lowered his nose beneath the surface to blow bubbles, then sucked eagerly at the refreshing liquid. Jonas only allowed Rebel a short drink, then pulled the blaze-faced bay's muzzle out of the spring.

"Not too much. You don't want to get too much cold water too fast, and end up colickin'. I'll let you have more soon as I rub you down."

Jonas dismounted. He yawned and stretched, then led his horse a short distance away from the spring, to where the grass wasn't quite as lush. The bay dropped his head and began cropping at the tough gramma stems. Rebel would be allowed to graze on the richer grass near the spring after he'd cooled down. There was a much used fire pit formed of blackened rocks, which had probably been there since the time of the Comanches.

"All I have to do is gather some downed branches and I'll be able to cook myself some bacon and beans tonight, Rebel. I'll do that soon as I take care of you. Looks like we both eat good tonight, pal."

Jonas removed the bridle from Rebel's head, slipping the headstall over his ears and sliding the bit from his mouth. He left the halter in place, but untied the lead rope from his saddle horn and dropped it to the ground. Rebel had been trained not to wander off when the rope was used as a ground hitch.

Jonas then pulled the saddle and bridle from his horse's back. He stood the saddle on end, and draped the blanket over it to dry out. A damp blanket rubbing on a horse's back could lead to a painful, crippling case of saddle sores. And a sore-backed horse was of no use to anyone. Jonas opened his saddlebags, removed a currycomb and hoof pick. He went to work, pushing the comb's stiff bristles deep into Rebel's sweat and dirt encrusted hide. The horse leaned hard into the brush, nickering with pleasure.

"I reckon that does feel good, eh boy?" Jonas said. "I figure I'll wash up some myself before I make supper. Gotta check and clean out the hole in my belly anyway. Doc Lynch wasn't lyin'. If it gets infected, I'm a goner. I'm about done brushing you. Lemme clean out your hooves and you can get the drink I promised you. You can chow down as much as you'd like after that."

Jonas used the hoof pick to clean dirt from the soles of Rebel's feet. Shod horses tended to gather more debris as they traveled, the shoes tending to trap and hold soil and bits of rock.

Jonas found a good-sized pebble lodged between the sole and frog of Rebel's off rear hoof. It resisted his efforts to pry it loose, but he finally managed to work it out. With a curse, he tossed it into the depths of the spring.

"That's one rock that'll never mebbe cripple a horse again. It's damn good luck that stone was smooth and round, not sharp-edged, Rebel. Even so, it would have bruised your frog or rubbed it raw if we hadn't stopped when we did. Lucky it musn't have been jammed in your hoof all that long, probably less than a half mile or so. Otherwise, you'd have started limpin' by now. I'll check that foot before we head out in the morning, just to be certain you haven't gone lame."

Jonas dropped the hoof to the dirt. Rebel immediately went to his knees and rolled to scratch his back, undoing much of Jonas's work. Jonas stood, exasperated, hands on his hips.

"Rebel, goldang you. All my brushing you was for naught. See if you get a treat tonight, horse."

With a snort, Rebel lunged to his feet. He shook himself off, then lowered his head and began munching on the tall, lush grass which surrounded the spring. He turned his rump to Jonas and switched his tail.

"I give up," Jonas muttered. "It's high time I got my own supper."

• • •

Jonas was starved, so he decided to make his meager supper of bacon, beans, and black coffee before washing up. He was halfway through eating when Rebel came up behind him, and shoved his right shoulder.

"I'm sorry, pal, but I didn't make any biscuits tonight," Jonas apologized to his horse. "I've got a chunk of hardtack in my pocket. Will you settle for that?"

Rebel bobbed his head, and tugged at Jonas's vest. He knew where his rider kept the treats. Jonas laughed, took the stale hardtack from his pocket, and gave it to his horse, who happily crunched down on the treat.

"You sure are spoiled, ya know that, ya old biscuit eater. But it's all right. You're a good pardner, and you've gotten me out of tough scrapes more than once. Besides, with Will back in Quitaque, you're the only one I have to talk with."

Jonas glanced up at the sky. The moon was well past its zenith.

"Soon as you finish that hardtack you'd best get some sleep, Rebel. It's gettin' close to midnight. I'm gonna finish my supper and turn in myself."

Rebel went back to his grazing. Jonas finished his supper, went to his saddlebags. He took out a clean cloth, one of the bandages Dr. Lynch had provided, and a bar of harsh yellow soap.

He walked over to the spring. He removed his shirt, then laid on his belly, taking a long drink of water, then dipping his face into the pool to soothe his sun scorched skin. He was startled by a voice behind him.

"Don't move, *hombre*. I've got my gun pointed at your back, and I can't miss. It's up to you whether you live or die tonight. I'm takin' your horse and all your gear."

Jonas cursed himself under his breath. How had he not heard the man sneaking up on him? It was a mistake even the rawest rookie wouldn't make. And why hadn't Rebel whinnied an alarm? All questions which could be answered later, if he lived long enough to answer them. For now, he'd have to play the hand he was dealt. And whoever was holding the gun on him held the high cards. He was damn lucky the gunman hadn't just shot him in the back and been done with it.

"You've got me dead to rights, Mister. I won't try anything."

"Smart decision. I'm leavin' you my animal. It's about done in, but it might get you to a ranch nearby."

"I wouldn't if I were you."

"How you gonna stop me?"

"Like this!"

Jonas whistled, rolled onto his back while pulling his Bowie knife out of its sheath. He had to make his throw by placing the sound of the horse thief's voice. Caught by surprise, the man triggered his gun without aiming. The bullet went over Jonas and skipped across the surface of the pool when the heavy knife took him in the chest. He stumbled back, at the same moment Rebel, coming in answer to Jonas's call, ran up. The horse lowered his head, hit the man in his back, and knocked him to the ground. He reared up and brought his front hooves down on the dying man's spine.

"Enough, Rebel! He's had enough!" Jonas ordered.

Rebel trotted up to him and nuzzled his cheek.

"Good boy. I'm all right. But where the hell were you gone? You usually warn me when we've got unwanted company?"

A gust of wind provided the answer. Jonas hadn't noticed the breeze picking up. The man who'd nearly succeeded in killing him, then taking his horse and possessions, had approached from downwind, keeping Rebel from scenting or hearing him or his horse, and Jonas from realizing he was in danger.

"Well, I'm still alive, and so are you, so I guess things worked out. Lemme take a look at this jasper and see if he's got any identification, or by chance might be a wanted fugitive."

Jonas rolled the man onto his back. He was in his late twenties, with dark brown hair and eyes, a scraggly beard, and a swarthy complexion.

Jonas didn't recall seeing his face or description on any wanted posters or in the Rangers Fugitive List. He pulled his knife from the man's chest and wiped it clean on the dead *hombre*'s shirt, then slid it back into its sheath. He went through the man's pockets, finding only a few bills and coins, a ragged billfold, a sack of Bull Durham, cigarette papers, and a small bottle containing matches.

"There's nothing on him, Rebel. Let's round up his horse. Mebbe we'll find something in the saddlebags."

From the dark, another horse gave a weak whinny. Rebel responded with one of his own. The other animal, an emaciated pinto gelding, emerged from behind some brush and walked up to Rebel. They sniffed noses and nickered, then pawed the dirt.

"Now I'm not sorry I killed that *hombre*," Jonas muttered. "Anyone who'd treat a horse like that deserves killin'."

He picked up the pinto's trailing reins and examined him. The horse was coated with dried sweat and dirt. Spur gouges marred his sides and flanks. His rump was cruelly cut where he had been whipped repeatedly.

"You're safe now, feller," Jonas assured the horse. "Lemme get the gear off of you. Nibble on some grass while I go through it. Then I'll rub you down and treat those cuts, best as I can."

Jonas uncinched the saddle, dropped it and the sweat-soaked blanket to the ground. He cursed the dead man when he removed the pinto's bridle and slid the bit out of the horse's mouth. The corners of his lips were rubbed raw by his rider pulling and yanking mercilessly on the reins. Jonas rubbed the horse's velvety nose.

"You eat and get a drink while I go through this stuff. Then I'll fix you up."

He wasn't concerned about the horse wandering off. Not with cool water and sweet grass at hand, plus Rebel for company. In addition, the poor, abused animal was too weak and exhausted to go on. Jonas was amazed the pinto was still upright. He must have more bottom than it appeared.

Jonas turned his attention to the saddle. One of the saddlebags contained some of the usual trail gear, a frying pan and coffee pot, Arbuckle's, bacon and beans, spare shirt and socks. He whistled when he opened the other bag and removed several bundles of wrapped yellowbacks, issued by the Anson City Bank. He thumbed through them, all of which were in denominations of ten or twenty dollars.

"Now I know why this here jasper was in such a hurry. There's got to be five hundred dollars in these bundles. Reckon I'll just put this *dinero* into my own saddlebags for safekeeping. Looks like I'll be goin' back to Sweetwater by way of

Anson City. They'll be plumb tickled to get this money back."

Once the money was safely secured, Jonas turned his attention back to the pinto. To gain the animal's confidence, he gave him a piece of hardtack, scratched his ears, then spoke soothingly to him while he worked. He combed as much dirt and sweat out of the horse's hide as possible, used a damp rag to clean out the animal's cuts and slashes, then coated those with salve. He turned the horse loose again, and decided the dead man could wait. He'd wrap him in his saddle blankets and tote him to Dickens, the nearest town, about twenty miles away, come morning. Right now, it was time to tend to his own hurts.

Jonas removed one of the bandages Dr. Lynch had given him, along with his styptic pencil and bottle of horse wound powder, from his saddlebags. He sat down, untied the old bandage from around his middle, wrapped it in a ball, and tossed it into the brush.

His wound had oozed some blood, but not enough to be concerned. Jonas took a bar of harsh yellow soap, worked up a lather with a damp cloth, washed his stomach and cleaned out the dried blood, then, feeling it would be more effective that the styptic pencil, used the wound powder to absorb and clot any more seepage, and keep the wound dry. He laughed as he filled his belly button to the rim.

"Guess I don't have to worry about putting enough medicine in that hole. My damn belly button's a natural container."

He placed the new bandage over the wound, tied that in place. He stood up and eased back into his shirt.

"Time to get some sleep. I'll just toss the blankets over that corpse and build up the fire a little. That'll keep any scavengers away."

Jonas covered the body, checked on both horses one more time, then rolled out his own blankets. He pulled off his boots and gun belt, leaving his six-gun and rifle within easy reach. He yawned and stretched, then slid under his blankets, using his saddle as a pillow. He placed his Stetson over his face, and within five minutes was softly snoring, fast asleep.

9

Jonas slept until an hour after sunrise the next morning. He made and ate a quick breakfast of biscuits and bacon, washed out the frying pan, dish, and coffee mug, and repacked his saddlebags. He also counted the yellowbacks, which totaled five hundred and fifty dollars. He rolled the dead man tightly in his blankets, then laid him belly down over his saddle and lashed him in place. The man's pinto snorted a little at having to carry the body, but didn't object very much. Jonas got his own gear on Rebel, then mounted up to continue his journey southward. Ordinarily, he wouldn't wear his badge in plain sight, but today it was pinned to his vest. Leading a horse carrying a dead man, he might run into someone who would try and shoot first, before asking any questions. The badge made clear his status as a Texas Ranger. While it wouldn't keep any *mal hombres* from trying to gun him down, he was prepared to handle those. Displaying his badge would at least keep honest folks honest.

Keeping the horses mostly at a walk, Jonas covered the twenty miles to Dickens in a little more than four hours, arriving in the town shortly after noon. The place could barely even be called a settlement, let alone a town. It consisted of a small trading post, which also served as a café and saloon, a blacksmith's shop, and a few houses. A hand lettered sign hanging on the trading post's door read *Closed from Noon to 3*. In the heat of the afternoon, no one was on the single street, the inhabitants having taken shelter from the merciless sun. Jonas reined up in front of the blacksmith's shop and dismounted.

"Howdy! Anyone around?"

A scruffy, medium sized brown dog rushed out of the smithy, growling and barking.

"Be right with you! Njal, keep quiet!" a voice answered from the back, in a heavy Scandinavian accent. The dog stopped barking and sat down, its tail wagging and tongue hanging out. A moment later, a burly, blonde haired, blue eyed, bare-chested man, holding a hammer and tongs, wearing canvas pants, heavy boots, and a leather apron came from the rear of the shop. He glanced at the badge pinned to Jonas's vest, then the body on the horse he was leading.

"Howdy. What can I do for you, Ranger? I'm Olaf Swenson. That's my boy's horse you're leadin', totin' that body. Bjorn'll sure be happy to see Pokey again. We figured he was gone for good. That the *hombre* who stole him under that blanket?"

"Seems as if," Jonas answered. "He tried to steal my horse. Bad mistake on his part. He paid for it."

"So I see. From the way it appears he treated my boy's horse, good riddance. He left another one behind that was in even worse shape. I nearly put it out of its misery, but my son begged me not to, so I decided to give it a chance. Plenty of hay, grain, and decent care and it seems to be comin' around just fine. I was gonna let Bjorn have that one, but he would never have stopped pinin' away for ol' Pokey. Pokey was a present from his grandpa, my wife's father. He was just a foal, and Bjorn only four, when he got Pokey. They've been growin' up together. My father-in-law passed away two years ago, so Pokey means something really special to all of us. I appreciate you bringing him back."

"Jonas Peterson. I'm on my way back to the Ranger post in Sweetwater. I was hoping to find a place to bury this body, then make a few more miles before nightfall. Any chance I can plant this man here in town? My horse could use new shoes all around, and I could use a good meal rather'n my bacon, beans, and biscuits. Then I'll be on my way. Need to cover some more ground before stoppin' for the night."

"There's a cemetery on the edge of town. I'll hustle up a couple of men and we'll take care of the burying this afternoon. I was just about to wash up and head over to the house for dinner. You'd be more than welcome to join us. My wife's a fine cook. I'll shoe your horse after we eat. First I'm gonna round up Bjorn and let him know his Pokey is back home. I can't wait to see the look on his face."

"I'll take the body off of him and hide it behind your smithy while you do that. There's no need for your boy to have to see it. I'll pull the gear off too. I reckon you can keep it for your trouble, along with the horse this jasper left you."

"Better do it quick, because once Bjorn finds out Pokey has come home, he'll be out here lickety-split."

"It'll only take me a minute. I'm just gonna dump him on the ground."

"I'll go rustle up my boy while you do that. And I'm really obliged for you bringing Pokey back."

"*Por nada*. I'm lucky I was still alive to bring him back. Must've been more tired than I realized when I made camp up at Roaring Springs last night, and got careless. I didn't hear that man ride up. Let him get the jump on me. Still haven't figured out why he didn't just plug me in the back before I even knew he was there. He had me dead to rights. Only reason I'm still here is he wasn't expectin' me to move quick as I did. That, and my horse finished him off. Rebel don't take kindly to most strangers."

"The Good Lord must have been watchin' over you too, Ranger. We'll say a prayer of thanks to Him for protecting you and leading you back to our door. We'll do that soon as we say Grace."

"I'm not much of a prayin' man, but I sure agree with you, and thanking God Almighty is the least I can do."

Swenson headed for the house, while Jonas led Pokey around the back of the smithy. He took the dead man off the horse, and dragged him up against the barn. He had just come back around to the front when a tow-headed whirlwind, running as fast as an eight-year-old boy's legs could carry him, came racing from the house. He crashed into Jonas so hard the impact drove most of the air from the Ranger's lungs, and nearly knocked him off his feet. Only the horse behind him kept him from falling backwards. The boy bounced off Jonas and wrapped his arms around the pinto's neck. Tears of happiness streamed down his cheeks as he hugged his horse, who was nickering with joy.

"Pokey. You came home. I never thought I'd see you again," the boy cried. "I'm never gonna let you out of my sight any more. I'll even sleep in the barn with you."

Swenson was right behind Bjorn, along with a strawberry blonde haired, light blue-eyed woman who was several months pregnant. She wore her hair in a circular braid on the back of her head, and was dressed in a loose fitting, blue checked cotton gingham dress, over which was a starched white apron.

"Bjorn, don't forget your manners," she said. "Thank the gentleman who found your horse and brought him back."

"It's all right, ma'am," Jonas said. "I know I'd be just as excited as your boy if my horse was lost and someone found him for me."

"Ranger, this is my wife Helga," Swenson said. "Helga, Ranger Jonas Peterson. And you've already met Bjorn, Ranger, although his greeting was a bit enthusiastic. I apologize."

"It's fine. And I'm pleased to make your acquaintance, Mrs. Swenson."

"I'm also pleased to meet you. Bjorn, you still need to thank Ranger Peterson for bringing Pokey home," Helga repeated. Like her husband, she had a strong Scandinavian accent, which gave her voice a pleasant, musical lilt.

"I know, Ma."

Bjorn held out his hand, which Jonas took and shook.

"Thanks, Ranger Peterson. Pokey is my bestest friend in the whole world. I'm sure glad you brought him home. And I'm sorry for runnin' into you."

"I know how you feel," Jonas said. "There's no harm done. Rebel is my best buddy. Pokey is going to need some extra care. The man who took him didn't treat him very well."

"I'll take good care of him. I promise. But Pa, what about Smokey? Can we still keep him?"

"Unless he was also stolen, and his owner is found and wants him back, yah."

To Jonas Swenson continued, "Smokey is the name Bjorn gave the horse which was left in Pokey's place. He's that steeldust gray in the corral. Bjorn, why don't you put Pokey in the corral with him, and give them both some hay. You can brush out Pokey and spend time with him after we eat dinner. It's going to get cold otherwise. Ranger Peterson, you'll join us, of course."

"I'm afraid we don't usually have meat for our noon meal," Helga said. "Just fresh vegetables from my garden. I've also made *Skoleboller*, Norwegian school bread. That's a sweet dough filled with vanilla custard, then covered in vanilla icing and dipped in coconut. It's quite filling, and still warm."

"Fresh vegetables and home-made bread? That sounds just fine, Mrs. Swenson. Far better than the bacon and beans I cook for myself. Mr. Swenson, is it all right if I put my horse in with the others?"

"Of course, Ranger. You may even spend the night if you'd like."

"It's a tempting offer, but I can still put a lot of miles behind me before dark. I have to get back to the Ranger post at Sweetwater as quickly as possible. There's no other Rangers there at the moment. My partner was hurt in a gunfight with a gang of bank robbers and murderers, so he had to remain in Quitaque to recuperate. But we did take care of that outfit, once and for all. They won't be committing any more crimes."

"I hope he'll have a complete recovery," Helga said.

"He will. He should be back to work in a couple of weeks."

"I'll pray for him, and you. Now, you'll want to wash up before eating. I'll set out some washcloths, towels, and soap while you get the horses put away. Bjorn, no taking shortcuts. Make certain your hands are clean. And behind your ears. There's so much dirt behind those I could grow potatoes there."

"Aw, gee, Ma."

"No clean hands, no *Skoleboller*."

"I know I'd clean up good for *Skoleboller*, and I've never even tasted it," Jonas said, with a laugh.

"Follow Ranger Peterson's example," Helga said. "By the time you've washed up dinner will be on the table."

A pump and wash bench was at the back of the house. Jonas, Swenson, and Bjorn scrubbed their hands and faces thoroughly, since Bjorn had warned Jonas even he would be checked by Helga, to make certain no traces of dirt remained under his fingernails or behind his ears. The table was brimming with bowls of carrots, black-eyed peas, pinto beans, corn, yellow squash, and cabbage. In the center of the table was a thick ceramic pitcher filled with milk from the Swenson's cow, and a platter covered with *Skoleboller.*

"It all looks and smells delicious," Jonas said.

"I hope you are hungry," Helga said. "I trust you won't mind there's no coffee. We all drink milk with dinner. Coffee is served at supper."

"I'm more than hungry. I'm famished. And milk will be just fine."

"That's goot. A man should have a hearty appetite after working hard. We always thank the Lord for His blessings before we eat. We always say the Grace in Norwegian, to honor our homeland. I hope you don't mind."

"Not at all."

Everyone folded their hands and bowed their heads, while Helga prayed the blessing.

"*Ve takker deg, Herre, for denne gode maten, familien var og gjesten var, Ranger Peterson. Vi takker deg ogsa for at du holdser Ranger Peterson trygg, og ber om din beskyttelse for ham og partneren hans. Amen.*"

"Now let's eat!" Bjorn exclaimed.

"I'm with you," Jonas said.

Jonas pushed himself back from the table and patted his stomach. He'd eaten until he was afraid the buttons on his denims would explode, fly across the kitchen, and take someone's eye out.

"Thank you so much for the meal, Mrs. Swenson. It's the best I've had in a month of Sundays."

"You're more than welcome," Helga answered. "I love to see folks enjoying my cooking and baking, but we get so few visitors here I don't often get the chance. Are you certain you wouldn't like just one more *Skoleboller*?"

"Thank you, but no. I'd purely love another one, but I've already had three. Any more and I'd burst."

"Let's go outside and have a smoke. We need to digest some of our meal before I shoe your horse," Swenson suggested.

"That's not a bad idea. But would you like some help cleaning up, Mrs. Swenson?" Jonas asked.

"Not at all. Men are only allowed in my kitchen to eat. They can't keep things as neat and tidy as I like them. Bjorn will help with the dishes. You and Olaf go ahead. I'll pack some food for you to take along, Ranger."

"You don't need to do that," Jonas protested.

"I want to, and I won't take no for an answer. Now shoo!"

"Yes'm."

Jonas and Swenson went outside, and sat on the

front steps. Swenson took out a sack of tobacco, a meerschaum pipe, and a match. Jonas got out his sack of Bull Durham, rolling papers, and separated a lucifer from its bundle. He rolled and lit a cigarette while Swenson filled his pipe, tamped down the tobacco, and lit it. Swenson took a long draw on the meerschaum before speaking.

"Ranger, I've been wondering about something ever since you showed up. You mind if I ask you a question?"

"No, go right ahead. I may not answer it, but I don't mind you asking."

"That dead man you brought in on Bjorn's horse. From the condition Pokey was in, and how badly he'd abused his own horse, it's obvious he just wasn't an ordinary traveler who was in a hurry. Am I right?"

"You are," Jonas answered. "His saddlebags held several bundles of ten and twenty dollars bank notes issued by the Anson City Bank. They added up to five hundred and fifty dollars. It's clear he robbed the bank, or another business or person. I have the money in my saddlebags."

"Yet you didn't mention that."

It wasn't an accusation, just a flat statement of fact.

"No, I didn't," Jonas admitted. "For a few reasons. First, I don't want word to get around there's a lone man on horseback carrying over five hundred dollars on him. That knowledge might be enough to tempt even an honest man into trying for it. Second, if you'd known about the robbery, you'd have mentioned it. Third, since the man came into town on a hard-ridden horse, then stole another one, it's plain the money wasn't stolen here in Dickens, because folks would be lookin' for it. No one gave me a second glance when I rode through town. So wherever the money was taken, it wasn't from around here. I'll take it to Anson City, return it to the bank there, then send out some telegrams to see if the same *hombre* who robbed it might've been involved in any other holdups, or where he might've come from. There might be a warrant out for his arrest. Does that answer your question?"

"It does. Although you can't be certain I wouldn't just stab you in the back, then dispose of your body. Or I could easily snap your neck with my bare hands. Or shoot you in the back as you ride off. It wouldn't be all that difficult to dispose of your body, without even my wife and son knowing. After all, you just met me. I have to say I admire your honesty, and your trust."

"I'm aware of all that," Jonas responded. "However, a lawman has to be a good judge of character. You don't strike me as the type. Of course, my gut feeling could be wrong, but I have a hunch you wouldn't keep that cash, even if I rode in here all shot up and fell out of my saddle, dead, with no witnesses to see you find and hold onto the *dinero*. I hope I'm not wrong."

"You're not, Ranger. Five hundred and fifty dollars is an awful lot of *kroner*, but I wasn't raised that way. Your secret is safe with me."

"I'm obliged."

"And my family will be eternally grateful to you for bringing Pokey back home. Soon as I finish my pipe I'll get to work on your horse."

Two hours later, Jonas was back in the saddle, ready to resume his journey. His saddlebags were stuffed with sandwiches and vegetables from Mrs. Swenson.

"You're certain you don't want to stay the night, and start out fresh in the morning?" she asked him.

Jonas shook his head.

"I just can't. I still have more'n two days until I reach Sweetwater, and that'll be hard ridin' all the way. Thanks to you, I have plenty of food to last me awhile. I'll travel until me'n Rebel are tired, then call it a night. Thanks again for your hospitality."

"Thank you for all you've done, Ranger," Swenson said. "Godspeed, and safe travels. Stop by anytime you're in the area. By then, Helga will have had her baby."

"I will," Jonas promised. "Bjorn, next time I

come by, I want to see Pokey and Smokey both all fat, sassy, and full of vinegar. I'm counting on you."

"They will be. You can be certain of that," Bjorn answered. "Hope you can come back real soon."

"I never know where the Rangers will send me, but I'm certain I'll be back this way, sooner or later. Time to get movin.' *Adios*."

He heeled Rebel into a slow jogtrot.

"So long, Ranger!" Bjorn called after him. He stood waving until Jonas was out of sight.

Jonas rode steadily until about ten that night. The rest of the trip to Sweetwater would be much like the first portion, over a semi-arid, level to rolling plain, with few water sources, and only scattered mesquites, junipers, cactus, and drought-tolerant desert grasses. Anson City would be the next real town he came to. Tonight would be a dry camp. He got the gear off Rebel, brushed him down, and gave the horse half the contents of his canteen.

"We'll find some water tomorrow, pal, I promise you. Go find something to munch on."

Rebel nuzzled Jonas's shoulder and nickered. He pawed at the saddlebags.

"Oh no you don't, horse. Those carrots and dried apples from the Swensons are for me, not you."

Rebel nickered more loudly, and pawed harder at the saddlebags.

"All right. One carrot and one apple, but that's all. There ain't much chance of us comin' across another place to buy supplies until we get home. There's still almost a hundred miles between here and the post, with no towns a'tall, just a few scattered ranches. *If* those haven't been abandoned during the dry spell we've been havin'. Lots of folks have given up, pulled up stakes, and moved on. Anson City's where you'll get a stall and decent meal."

Jonas took an apple and carrot from his saddlebags, and fed them to Rebel. After he had munched on those, the bay nosed the saddlebags, hoping for more.

"I'm sorry, boy, but we've got to make what little we've got last until we reach Anson City. Even if I scare up a jackrabbit or quail for my supper, that won't do you any good."

He slapped Rebel fondly on the shoulder.

"G'wan, go graze and get some rest. We'll be hittin' the trail again by sunup."

Jonas ate his own supper, then rolled out his blankets. The night was still warm, with some humidity, so he just laid atop them, his head pillowed on his saddle.

Two more days. That's all I need, two more days.

10

The next day started out already hot and humid. The sun rose brassily over the shimmering plains. For a split second, Jonas didn't believe his eyes. When the top edge of the sun just touched the eastern horizon, a brilliant green flash appeared, then was gone just as quickly.

"What in the blue blazes was that?" he exclaimed. "Must've been the heat playin' tricks on my eyes." He didn't know he'd just seen an extremely rare atmospheric phenomenon known to astronomers as the "green flash." Conditions had to be just right for it to occur. It required a true horizon, clear skies, and haze free air. The unusual event was therefore seen most often on the ocean, a flat plain, or from a mountaintop with a clear view of the surrounding area. It occurred at either sunrise or sunset, as the upper edge of the sun just topped or went below the horizon. When the sun was rising or setting, it scattered all the visible to the human eye wavelengths of light. When the sun is low on the horizon, its light has to travel through more of the atmosphere, meaning it scatters all the wavelengths, so the longer wavelengths of reds, yellows, and oranges appear, blocking out the greens, blues, and violets. As it climbs higher in the sky, the long wavelength colors become less scattered, while the short blue and violet wavelengths are still bounced around by the atmosphere. Violet is on the edge of the visible human spectrum, and is harder to see, so the sky appears blue. Green, being on the cusp of the longer wavelengths, only appears for a moment, when the conditions are aligned perfectly. It is only scattered for less than a second, so the green flash is an elusive quarry for sky watchers.

Jonas shook his head, then whistled up Rebel. He poured half the remaining water from his canteen into his hat, and let his horse suck that down greedily. He ate a stale piece of hardtack and half a carrot for his breakfast, giving the other half to Rebel. After taking just a sip of water to moisten his mouth, Jonas saddled and bridled Rebel, pulled himself into the saddle, and pointed his horse south once again. Despite the heat, he hoped to cover fifty miles this day. If he could manage that distance, it would make the final days' push to Anson City and Sweetwater that much shorter.

The heat intensified rapidly as the morning wore on. A gray haze obscured the sky, lowering and thickening as noon grew near. A southeast breeze, laden with moisture from the Gulf of Mexico, picked up. Jonas stopped several times to rest his weary horse. They were both drenched with sweat. It lathered Rebel's bay coat, streaked his legs, dripped from his belly and muzzle. It plastered Jonas's shirt to his back, made dark circles under his armpits, and trickled down his chest. It flowed down his forehead, over his cheeks and nose, dripping through his beard and from his chin. No matter how many times he removed his hat to wipe his brow and remove sweat from the Stetson's sweatband, it was soaked again within minutes. The sun disappeared behind clouds that had grown from white and puffy to dark and threatening, their bellies black and heavy with moisture. The thick air was even more miserable than the sun beating down.

"We're due for one whopper of a storm, Rebel, and there's no place to seek shelter from it. We're sittin' ducks out here. We're just gonna have to keep moving, and hope we come across a farmhouse or ranch, or mebbe an abandoned line shack. Hell, I'd even settle for a bank we could huddle against and at least keep out of the wind that's comin', sure as shootin'. I just hope a twister doesn't blow up."

Rebel, who was usually calm, seldom frightened even in the worst of circumstances, such as the middle of a running gunfight, tossed his head and whickered nervously.

"I know. I'm worried too, pal," Jonas told him, patting his neck. "But look on the bright side. If it does rain, we won't have to worry about findin' water."

Rebel snorted again, twisted his neck to look back at Jonas, and rolled his eyes.

"Yeah, you're right. That ain't much comfort."

The first flash of lightning lit the northwest sky, and a muted rumble of thunder sounded a few minutes later, both still far off. Jonas untied his yellow oilskin slicker from the cantle of his saddle and pulled it on. The heavy garment trapped his body's perspiration, only adding to his misery.

"Let's hope the Good Lord is watching over us, and leads us to shelter before the storm really hits, pardner."

Rebel shook his head, as if agreeing with his rider.

Twenty minutes later, the first large, cold drops of rain, mixed with hail, began falling, spattering the ground, bouncing off Jonas's hat and slicker, stinging Rebel's hide. The southeasterly wind picked up, blowing steadily at over thirty miles per hour, with higher gusts, taunting Jonas's efforts to keep moving as he leaned into it, urging Rebel on. Lightning flashed and thunder rumbled more frequently now, each flash and boom louder, and nearer together.

The storm continued to worsen, copious amounts of rain coming down so hard visibility was less than a hundred feet, the lightning and thunder practically continuous. Brighter flashes and loud crackles indicated when a bolt hit a nearby tree, a ledge, or a patch of ground. The road turned to mud, sucking at every hoof step Rebel made. In some spots it was already so deep the horse had to struggle to pull his foot out of the fetlock deep, clinging mud. Jonas whispered a prayer of thanks he had replaced Rebel's shoes back in Dickens. If he hadn't, the mud would have been certain to pull one or more of them off.

"This is a real gully washer, Rebel. We've got to find somewhere to hole up right quick, before one of those lightning bolts finds *us*. Or worse, since I can't see or hear a doggone thing ahead of us, we might stumble into a flooded wash before we saw it, and end up drowning. And this road's turnin' into a quagmire. I can't chance you mebbe bowing a tendon or snapping a leg bone in this muck. Anything at all that looks it might provide any shelter, even a bit, we're gonna have to chance it."

Jonas had to shout to be heard over the wind, which snatched his words away as soon as they passed through his lips. He couldn't even be certain Rebel heard him. Head down, the sturdy little bay mustang plodded doggedly on. He wouldn't quit until Jonas ordered him to stop, or his heart gave out.

Jonas's hope and prayers that the storm would blow over quickly, like so many thunderstorms on the plains did, proved futile. This one kept intensifying, the rain and hail coming down in wind driven sheets, the almost constant lightning blinding, the rumbling and growling of the thunder incessant. Rebel stopped several times, unable to make any headway against the howling winds. Jonas rode slumped in the saddle, exhausted, soaked even with the protection of his pulled-low hat and slicker. He was just about to give up when a flash of lightning revealed a ramshackle, abandoned cabin just a few yards ahead.

"Looks like the Lord's answered our prayers, Rebel! We might just come outta this storm with our hides intact after all."

He urged his weary gelding into a trot. When they reached the cabin, the door was already ajar, hanging by one hinge. Jonas didn't dismount, just rode Rebel straight inside. He slid off his horse, and, overcome with weariness, leaned against Rebel for support as he looked around the cabin. The roof had several holes, so it leaked like a sieve. The windows were all long gone, only the empty frames remaining. There was a table, single chair, and a wood stove, its pipe fallen away. In one corner was a bunk, with a rodent-chewed mattress. Lying on the bunk were the bleached bones of the cabin's last occupant. Jonas gave a start when he spotted the skeleton, which had a bullet hole in its breastbone. For a minute, he thought about pushing on. Still, the walls broke the force of the wind, the chair could be broken up for firewood, the stove, even without its pipe, could be used since any smoke would rise through the holes in the roof, and make its way outside. Part of the cabin's interior, despite the leaks, remained dry. Most important, both Jonas and his horse had reached the limits of their endurance. Rebel was so worn out even the sight of the skeleton didn't faze him. Attempting to keep fighting the storm would only mean death.

"Looks like we ride things out here, Rebel," he told the horse. He pulled the gear off Rebel, placed it in a dry corner, then rubbed him down. He opened the stove, finding there was still some kindling inside. There were also two lengths of firewood alongside it. They were damp, but once the kindling took hold, they should burn. The chair would then become sufficient firewood until conditions allowed travel again.

Jonas took out a match, lit it, and touched it to the kindling. It took three tries before the slivers of wood took hold sufficiently to keep burning. Jonas then put one chunk of firewood in the stove, waited until that caught, then added the second and closed the door. Smoke rose from where the stove pipe had been attached, rose to the roof, formed a haze there, gradually worked its way through the holes in the roof and the glassless windows, leaving the air inside breathable. Jonas took off his boots and socks, leaving them in front of the stove to dry. His blankets were soaked, so he placed those on the side of the table nearest the fire, allowing them to hang over the edge where the fire would dry them. He kept the rest of his wet clothes on, except for his hat and bandanna, which he put on top of his blankets. Rebel, too exhausted to care about food or water, was huddled in a corner of the cabin, standing head low and spraddle-legged, sleeping. Jonas climbed onto the table, stretched out on his back, and immediately fell asleep. He awoke once during the night when the fire died down. The storm still raged. Jonas broke up the chair, using its wood to replenish the fire. Once that was done, he climbed back onto the table, and went right back to sleep.

The next morning, the storm had blown itself out. The air was cool and crisp. It held an earthy tang from the left behind moisture and damp earth. The sun's rays coming through the holes in the cabin's roof weren't what awakened Jonas, however. It was the roar of close by rushing water, growing louder by the minute.

Jonas rolled off the table and hurried outside. Two hundred feet beyond the cabin was a normally dry wash, which had been impossible to see or hear over the previous might's storm. Now the wash was bank full of muddy, roiling, debris filled water. The water was still rising, threatening to overtop its banks and swamp the cabin very soon.

Jonas raced back inside, grabbed his boots and socks, pulled the neckerchief over his ears and down around his neck, jammed his hat on his head. He threw the saddle and bridle on Rebel's back, then gathered his blankets and tossed them over his gear.

"C'mon, pal, we don't have any time to waste."

He took Rebel's lead rope and led him outside. The floodwaters had now overflowed the wash and were rushing around the cabin. Jonas got away from it and to higher ground as fast as he could move. He stopped, out of breath, but was now a good four feet above the water.

He gasped for breath.

"Looks like we're gonna be here for a spell, Rebel. I doubt the water'll get much higher, since the rain's stopped, but if it does we can just move back some more. Usually flash floods like this go down as quick as they come up."

Rebel snorted, then dropped his nose to the grass. He began to graze. Jonas removed the pile of gear from the horse's back, then sat down to pull on his socks and boots. He also remembered he hadn't cleaned his wound and changed the bandage, so he did that. He rolled and lit a cigarette, then watched the water as it continued to rise.

The water stopped rising when it reached a depth of more than two feet around the cabin. The old structure couldn't withstand the pressure of the swift current for very long. It creaked and groaned, then its walls separated. It collapsed into the flood, which pulled it toward the deeper water in the wash itself. It continued disintegrating, pieces bobbing along the surface. The mattress rose to the surface of the water, the skeleton still lying atop it. When it drifted into a whirlpool, the waterlogged mattress was quickly pulled under again. The skeleton, also trapped in the swirling water, spun crazily, until only one hand was visible above the surface. The hand also soon sank, but not before waving as if it were bidding *adieu* to this world. Then, it was gone.

11

Jonas had to wait a full day for the floodwaters to subside and the sandy soil in the wash dried out sufficiently so that he and Rebel might not bog down in quicksand. With both he and his horse still tired and sore from their exertions in surviving the storm, Jonas didn't hurry as he'd planned. He took three full days to cover the hundred miles to Anson City. It was full dark when he rode into the town.

"I know it's a little late, Rebel, but the streets are awful empty. There doesn't seem to be anyone about. Something's wrong here. Soon as I find the marshal's or the county sheriff's office and turn this money over to one of them, I'll get you a stall at the livery stable and me a room at the hotel. Then I'll do some snoopin' around, see if I can find out anything."

Rebel snorted and shook his head. As Jonas continued down the street, it seemed even more ominous to him that no one was walking around. Most of the businesses were closed, which was not unexpected this late in the evening, but to see not a single person on the sidewalks, nor any horses tied to the hitching rails, was most unusual.

Jonas came to the Anson City Marshal's Office

first. The building was dark. He dismounted and knocked on the door. No one answered. He tried the door, found it open. He struck a match, and lit a coal oil lamp he found on a desk. The place was deserted, and appeared to have been for quite some time. Bullet holes in the back wall, a tipped over chair, and a large pool of dried blood on the floor around the chair indicated someone had been shot and died in this room. Jonas blew out the lamp and retreated back to the street. Rebel looked at him questioningly, his ears pricked sharply forward. He whickered softly.

"I don't know what's happened hereabouts, but we've gotta be careful, pal," he told the bay, stroking the horse's velvety muzzle to reassure him. "Mebbe we can get some answers at the sheriff's office."

The Jones County Sheriff's Office and Courthouse was at the other end of town. It took Jonas only a few minutes to reach it. Once again, he dismounted, looped Rebel's reins around the tooth-scarred hitch rail, and went inside. There was only one person on duty, an elderly deputy. He looked around nervously when Jonas walked in.

"Evenin', stranger. What might I do for you?"

"That depends," Jonas answered. "Are you the man in charge tonight?"

The deputy lifted his hat, ran a hand through his thin gray hair, and dropped the hat back in place. He gazed at Jonas through clouded blue eyes.

"I am, but if you're lookin' for help, you won't find any here. Try the marshal's office."

"I already have. No one there. It sure looked as if no one was comin' back, neither. Appears someone was shot there, but I'm guessin' you already know that. Is the sheriff around?"

"The sheriff lit a shuck outta here three weeks ago. Right after the city marshal was gunned down. His deputy, too. And the other two county deputies."

"Four lawmen murdered in cold blood?"

"That's right."

"You'd better give me the entire story. What's your name, Deputy? And why are you still here?"

"The name's Tom Carlson. Only reason I'm still in town and above ground is the Wilson bunch knows I'm too old and scared to do anything about them. They let me keep my badge, and what little dignity I have left, as long as I leave 'em alone. I'd quit, but my wife is ailin', and I need the pay from the county for the doctor, and Matilda's medicines."

"The Wilson bunch? You mean Frank Wilson and his gang? They've been raisin' Hell all over the Southwest for far too long."

"All five of them. Each one meaner than the other."

"No one's tried to stop them?"

"They did. I just told you what happened to those men."

"I mean besides the law."

"Most folks are too scared to fight back. And a lot of them figure it's none of their affair, as long as they're left alone. No one dares to try and ride for help. The telegraph office was wrecked by the gang, and we ain't on a stage line, so it isn't all that often we get visitors. No doubt word's gotten around to keep out of Anson City. If I were you, I'd just keep on goin'. The Wilson bunch already know you're here. They're just watchin' you, and bidin' their time. Mebbe you'll get lucky and they'll leave you ride on."

Jonas shook his head.

"That won't happen, and you know it. They might not gun me down right in the middle of the street here in town, but they'll ambush me soon as I'm far enough away no one'll see what happens. You said you don't get any visitors. Well, you've got one right now. Texas Ranger Jonas Peterson. I reckon it's up to me to bring the Wilson outfit's reign of terror to an end. Right here and now. Tonight."

Jonas took his badge from his pocket and pinned it to his vest.

Carlson stared at the silver star in silver circle, which glittered in the dim lamplight.

"You're a Ranger? You're goin' after them by yourself?"

"It seems like the only choice I have, unless you want to lend a hand."

"Ranger, I'd only be in your way. I was a good lawman back in my day. But that's a long time ago. I can't chance anything happening to me and my Hildy being left all alone in this world. If that makes me a coward, I'm sorry."

"You needn't be. You sticking around rather than leaving with your tail tucked between your legs like the sheriff did makes you a braver man than he'll ever be. Where's the gang right now?"

"At the Alhambra Saloon. On Cross Street, three blocks south of here. They've made the place their headquarters. Mike Johnson, he's the owner, doesn't mind. He follows their orders and takes their money."

"There's no point in wastin' any more time."

Jonas walked behind the deputy's desk and removed two double-barreled ten gauge sawed off shotguns from the rack. He cocked the hammers on both Remingtons.

"You got more shells for these, Deputy?"

"In the bottom left hand desk drawer."

Jonas opened the drawer and removed as many shotgun shells as he could shove into his pockets.

"If I don't come back, try'n get word to Ranger Headquarters in Austin about what happened. Also my pardner, Will Kirkpatrick, who's in Quitaque right now, but'll be headed back to the Ranger post in Sweetwater in a few days. Oh, one more thing. I've got five hundred and fifty dollars in brand new bank notes issued by the Anson City Bank in my saddlebags. I found them on an *hombre* who tried to steal my horse. He'd ridden his most to death, plus he tried to kill me, so I'm positive those notes are stolen. If you can figure out who the rightful owner is and return them to him, I'd be obliged."

"I have an idea who they belong to. If I'm wrong, Silas Canby at the bank will know. The trick will be not letting the Wilson gang find out about that money. They'll figure it'll be easy pickin's."

"If I can pull this off, the Wilson gang will be finished for good after tonight. Wish me luck."

"Good luck, Ranger. And may God protect you."

"Thanks, Deputy."

Jonas left Rebel tied in front of the sheriff's office. Much as he, as most men born to the saddle did, hated walking, he'd have a far better chance of reaching the Alhambra Saloon undetected than by riding. Even if he could manage to silence the rattling of the bit and creaking of saddle leather, in the still night air Rebel's steps would sound as loud as a fire bell sounding the alarm. Besides, leaving his mustang at the sheriff's office would keep the horse out of danger when the shooting started. Jonas had no illusions about his chances of coming out of this fight alive. A snowball in the desert in August faced better odds.

Jonas had removed his spurs to prevent their jangling from giving him away. He edged along the buildings, keeping to the shadows as much as possible. He had no way of knowing for certain he wasn't already being watched. A bullet blasting from a side alley could end his life at any moment. One thing that was in his favor was the new moon, so the only light was that of the stars, and light spilling from an occasional window lit by a turned low coal oil lamp. He turned onto Cross Street. The light glowing from the door and windows of the Alhambra was in stark contrast to the otherwise near total darkness. Jonas edged along the front wall of the building. He ducked low to get past the window, then stood next to the door, his back to the wall, listening. He dearly wanted to chance looking through the window to see how many men were in the place, but didn't dare. From what he could ascertain from listening, there didn't appear to be more than a dozen or so people in the saloon. Five of those would be the members of the Wilson gang. The others would most likely be their friends, or those who had somehow made a deal with the devil to remain unmolested by the murderous bunch. The employees of the saloon wouldn't take a hand in the upcoming fight. Or if they did, it would be to help the outlaw gang.

Jonas took a deep breath and swallowed hard. He burst through the batwings, dropping his right-hand shotgun to the floor.

"Texas Ranger! Don't anyone move. You're all under arrest."

The men reacted as he'd expected, grabbing for their guns as they spun to face him. Three percentage girls screamed and ran for safety, as did two or three patrons. The outlaws themselves were pulling their revolvers from their holsters and bringing them level. Jonas fired both barrels of the shotgun he still held. Red spurted from the shirts of two outlaws as the spreading heavy buckshot ripped into their chests and stomachs. Knowing he'd made a good hit, with no time to hesitate Jonas didn't wait to watch them fall. He dropped the empty Remington, dove to the floor, grabbed the second shotgun where it had fallen, aimed, pulled the triggers, and cut the legs out from under two more men. He tossed aside the empty Remington and pulled his .44 Smith and Wesson from its holster.

Frank Wilson was still unscathed. He'd jumped to his feet when Jonas burst in, dumping the peroxide blonde, full-figured percentage girl on his lap to the floor. The outlaw boss was a disgraced politician, a former state senator who'd turned to violent crime after being forced out of office. Wilson was a heavy set man in his late forties or early fifties, with reddish orange hair he wore long and swept back over his scalp in a vain and futile attempt to conceal the fact he was mostly bald. His light brown eyes glared at Jonas in an expression of pure hatred. His complexion was sallow, his face heavy jowled, giving him an unhealthy appearance. However, he moved surprisingly quickly for a man of his bulk and age. He has his gun out and aimed at Jonas before the Ranger could bring his own revolver into play. Jonas had no time to stop Wilson from putting a bullet into his brain. He braced himself for the impact of hot lead.

A shot from outside shattered the window glass and plowed into Wilson's chest just as he pulled the trigger. His aim was spoiled by the impact. His shot went high, the bullet burying itself in the wall three feet over Jonas. Wilson staggered, but remained upright, a bright red splotch staining his shirtfront. Jonas fired his own gun, the bullet hitting Wilson in his substantial gut. Three more bullets came through the window. Crimson polka dots on Wilson's white shirt showed where each slug had hit. He collapsed in a heap, five bullets in his chest and belly. His body quivered in its death throes.

Mike Johnson, the Alhambra's owner, reached for the shotgun he kept behind the bar. Jonas put a bullet into the wood just below the bar's countertop, splintering it.

"I wouldn't do that if I were you. Keep your

hands where I can see them. That goes for the rest of you. Get your hands in the air and keep 'em away from your guns. Unless you want to end up like these others."

Johnson held his hands up to show they were empty, then laid them flat on the mahogany.

"I'd take the Ranger's advice, boys, bein' as I'm backing his play," Deputy Carlson called from outside. "You all right, Ranger?"

"Thanks to you I am . . . Tom," Jonas answered.

"I'm comin' right in."

Keeping his gun aimed at the men still standing, Jonas got to his feet. Carlson pushed his way through the batwings. He surveyed the gruesome scene. Five men lay dead or dying. The blonde percentage girl was clutching Wilson's body and sobbing. The others in the room were huddled in a back corner. It was obvious they wanted no part of this fight. Not after seeing four vicious killers die at the hands of one man, their leader cut down by the same man, with the help of an old, long past his prime deputy sheriff with poor eyesight.

"I thought you didn't want to take part in this," Jonas said.

"At first I didn't. But I realized I couldn't live with myself if I hadn't. Matilda would have been ashamed of me, too. So soon as you went out the office door I decided to follow you. It worked out better this way. More element of surprise, plus you weren't worried about me. Sorry for surprisin' you like this."

"I wish more men would," Jonas answered. "I'm certainly happy you decided to join the dance. I suppose we'd better start cleaning up this mess. Is there a doctor in town?"

"There is. Doc Twombley. He'll have heard the ruckus, and be on his way. Not that any of these men'll need a doctor."

The four men Jonas shot had breathed their last. The first two had died almost instantly from the massive damage the buckshot did to their internal organs. The other two had died of shock and massive blood loss from their wounds. The lead pellets had shredded their legs, tearing apart flesh, muscle, and bone. The ten gauge shot had practically amputated their limbs. Frank Wilson had been harder to kill, but he was indeed dead.

"You mind if I start first, Ranger?"

"Jonas. Be my guest."

Carlson pointed his gun at Mike Johnson's chest.

"I'm obliged. Mister Mayor, you're under arrest. Reach for the ceiling. Try anything, and you'll die where you stand. I'd purely love to sink a couple of bullets into you."

"Me? Why am I under arrest?"

Despite his protest, Johnson raised his hands shoulder high. He knew the deputy would do exactly what he threatened.

"For starters, harboring fugitives from the law. Tack on bribery, both accepting bribes and paying bribes. You've been allowing outlaws free rein in this town for a long time. When the *hombres* Ranger Patterson finished off here tonight killed the marshal, three deputies, and ran the sheriff out of town, I knew I had to put a stop to your corrupting the office of mayor, and swindling the honest citizens of Anson City. I was just bidin' my time. I was too much of a coward to try'n handle this bunch by myself, and I knew it'd be plumb suicide to even try. The Ranger here finally got me off my sorry butt and gave me some backbone again. I told him he was on his own, but then I realized helpin' him was my only chance to get my self-respect back, and to be a man again. First thing tomorrow I'll be issuing a warrant for that useless Sheriff Zeke Talbot's arrest. Dereliction of duty, and also taking bribes. Anson City couldn't have become an outlaw haven without the county sheriff being in cahoots with you and the renegades. I also plan on charging both of you with being accessories to murder, in the deaths of four good lawmen. There's no doubt of even more charges to follow, but those'll do for starters."

"You can't do that. I'll have your badge."

"That won't work, Mister Mayor. I'm the only Jones County lawman left, which means I'm in charge. The sheriff was elected by the citizens of the county, and I was appointed a county deputy by him. I don't work for you, or Anson City. You have no authority to fire me. Soon as we clean up this here mess, I'm gonna round up some of your cronies. Y'all can share cells. It'll be nice and cozy for each and every one of you blood suckin' parasites. Would you give me a hand with that, Ranger?"

"I'll be more than happy to. The Rangers were sent up here to clean up this entire territory, and that's what we're gonna do. Seems as if you'n me might've just made a good dent in the problem."

"You won't have me behind bars for long," Johnson said. "You both committed cold blooded murder here tonight, especially you, Ranger, damn you to Hell. You came in shooting. You didn't fight fair. You didn't give those men any opportunity to give themselves up."

"I called out 'Texas Ranger. You're under arrest'," Jonas retorted. "Not one of those men even thought of surrendering. They all went for their guns. As far as fighting fair, what do you think this is, some kind of dime novel, where everyone, even the bad guys, plays by the rules, whatever those are supposed to be? You expected me to come in here to face down a gang of murderous cutthroats with only a six-gun? And with it still in its holster, to boot? What do you think I am, some kind of a damn fool? Frank Wilson and his men were wanted for murders, robberies, and assaults in four states and three territories. I wasn't about to let them get the drop on me. They would all have been hung if they went to trial, and clearly they had no intention of being captured. And there's no judge in Texas who'd sign a warrant for my arrest, nor for Deputy Carlson's. Your empty threats don't worry me none."

Jonas removed his handcuffs from their case on his gun belt.

"Mayor, turn around and put your hands behind your back," he ordered. "Deputy, keep him covered while I cuff him. Anyone else in here you intend to arrest, or who might try to gun us down from an alley on our way to the jail?"

"Not here, these boys are regulars from some of the ranches outside of town, but there's a few others I'm gonna rouse from their beds. It's time to shake up this town, but good. The honest folks here have been cowed by outlaws for far too long. That's about to change."

While Jonas was placing Anson City's mayor in handcuffs, an elderly man, gray haired and green eyed, stooped with age, carrying a battered black leather medical bag, entered the saloon. He glanced at the bodies and let out a shrill whistle.

"Tom, what in the blue blazes happened in here? It seems like my services aren't needed."

"Just to pronounce the men are all dead, write up the certificates, and do a quick inquest, Cyrus."

Carlson nodded toward Jonas.

"This here's Texas Ranger Jonas Peterson. He didn't ride into town lookin' for trouble, hell, he wasn't even aware of the problems we've had in Anson City, but he sure found out, and took care of the situation right quick. Ranger, this here's the town doc, Cyrus Twombley. He's a right decent *medico*."

"Doctor, sorry to cause you such a mess," Jonas said.

"Ranger, if it rids this town of ruffians like the Wilson bunch, make as many messes as you'd like. I'll need some help getting the bodies down to my office. I reckon we can let Clete Cleveland sleep until morning. He's the undertaker, Ranger."

"Understood," Jonas said. "The rest of you men, give Doc Twombley a hand gettin' these bodies out of here. Any of you who aren't needed, go on home."

Twombley walked over to Wilson's body.

"Lula Mae, please get out of my way," he told the blonde. "There's nothing you can do for him."

"You killed Frank, Deputy," Lula Mas screeched, still huddled over Wilson's corpse. "He was the best lover I've ever had. He treated me real fine, like a high class lady."

"You'll find another one before long, Lula Mae. You always do."

"Carlson, you son of a bitch!"

Lula Mae rolled away from Wilson, snatched a two shot Derringer from her cleavage, and got off one quick shot, which clipped the deputy's left arm. Before she could fire again, Jonas shot her. The bullet he intended for her shoulder instead went through her neck, tearing through her windpipe, cutting her jugular in two. The slug exited her neck and thudded into Wilson's dead body. Lula Mae slumped over Wilson, her blood mingling with his.

"You all right, Tom?" Jonas asked.

"Yeah, just need the doc to patch me up. I was real lucky."

"Damn, I hate shootin' a lady," Jonas cursed.

"Lula Mae Riley might've been a woman, but she was no lady," Carlson said. "She'd have shot down the both of us without even blinking an eye. You did what you had to do."

"That still doesn't make me feel any better."

"It should. We're both still alive, and she's dead, which is all that matters, leastwise as far as I'm concerned. It could've turned out the other way around. Think on that."

"I reckon I don't need to," Jonas conceded. "Let's just get outta here."

"Do you want me to look at you here or down at my office, Tom?" Twombley asked.

"I can hold on until we get the bodies out of here and the place locked up," Carlson answered. "I'm hardly even bleeding."

• • •

Once they reached Doctor Twombley's office, the dead were placed in a shed out back. Twombley cleaned out Deputy Carlson's wound, took three stitches to hold the edges together, then dressed and bandaged it. Jonas also had the doctor examine his belly button wound. Twombley declared it was just about healed, and would need no further treatment.

As soon as they were they were done at the doctor's, Jonas appointed Carlson a Special Texas Ranger and Acting Sheriff of Jones County. He declined Carlson's offer of a bunk at the county jail for the night. He assisted Carlson as the deputy arrested and jailed seven more men he believed were involved in protecting the criminals who had made Anson City a safe haven for their ilk. It was close to one in the morning by the time they were finished. Instead of staying with the deputy, Jonas took Rebel to a nearby livery stable. He had to awaken the owner, and remained with his horse until he was certain the patient, long suffering mustang had been fed, watered, and rubbed down. Once certain Rebel's needs were tended to, he walked to the nearby Star Hotel to obtain a room for himself. The desk clerk was sleeping in his chair behind the front counter when he walked in. He never woke as Jonas walked up to the desk.

Jonas banged hard on the desk bell, startling

the man so he nearly fell over backwards. He managed to catch his balance before hitting the floor, then stood up and glared at the newcomer.

"What the hell do you want, Mister?"

"Is that any way to welcome a customer?" Jonas answered. He pointed to the silver star in silver circle badge pinned to his vest.

"Texas Ranger. Name's Jonas Peterson. I need a room for the next two nights."

"Ranger, huh? I'm Morton Handy, this hotel's owner. I'm afraid we're full up."

Jonas looked at the pigeonholes behind the desk. More than half of them held room keys hanging from hooks.

"It damn sure doesn't look like it. Listen close Mister Handy, because I'm only gonna say this once. I've been on the trail for days. This was just supposed to be a quick stop. Instead, I ride into town and find it's bein' run by outlaws. Me'n Deputy Carlson cleared out a whole bunch of those *hombres* tonight. Come daylight, we'll be looking to round up the rest of the snakes in this here town. I'm dead tired, just tangled with a bunch of *hombres* that tried their dangdest to kill me, and I need sleep. So like it or not, you're gonna give me a room. *Pronto*."

Handy swallowed hard. Beads of sweat popped out on his forehead. He stuck a finger under his collar to loosen it.

"All right, Ranger, you've made your point. I don't suppose the gunfire I heard earlier was connected to you."

"It was. If the Wilson gang was staying at this establishment, you now have even more empty rooms. Their next stay will be a permanent one, in cemetery plots."

"You mean they're all dead?"

"As a fish out of water for three days."

Hardy scowled.

"They still owe me for the rooms."

"I wouldn't count on collecting that cash. Do I get a room, or not?"

"I can scrounge one up."

Hardy turned and removed a key from its hook.

"Here you go, Ranger. Room 110. Down the corridor to the right. It's halfway down, on the left side. I'm certain you'll find it satisfactory. The Star is the finest hostelry in Anson City."

"It's got a bed with clean pillows, sheets and blankets, right?"

"Indeed it does. You'll also find a pitcher of water, and a basin, if you'd like to wash up."

"Then it'll be satisfactory."

"The rate's a dollar per night. If you'll just pay the charge and sign the register, I'll give you your key."

Handy turned the register so Jonas could check

in. Jonas scrawled his signature in the proffered book, then took two silver dollars from his pocket and placed them on the counter.

"Thank you, Ranger Peterson," Hardy said. "If you need anything at all just let me know. If you're looking for breakfast later this morning the Anson Center Café is just across the street. They serve decent food at reasonable prices."

"Thanks for the advice. There is one thing, I guess," Jonas answered. "Deputy Carlson informed me the city's mayor resides here at this hotel."

"Mayor Johnson? That's correct. He stays in our third-floor penthouse suite."

"That sounds mighty expensive for a small city's mayor."

Hardy flushed.

"Well, you see, um, he doesn't exactly, um, pay the entire cost of the suite. He, how shall I put this, he shares the accommodations with *Mademoiselle* Charlene de la Croix. She's a singer, or a *chanteuse* as she calls herself, at the Anson City Opera House."

"Then when you see *Mademoiselle* de la Croix, you need to inform her she will now be the sole occupant of the suite. Mayor Johnson has a new residence, the Iron Bar Hotel. Otherwise known as the Jones County Jail. Also, if there's even a hint that you've been making, how shall *I* put this, special arrangements for the mayor and his outlaw friends, you might be joining him. Have a good night."

Jonas left Handy staring slack-jawed at his back. He found his room, went inside, locked the door behind him. He shoved a chair under the doorknob for extra security, removed his boots, and fell face down on the bed. He was asleep as soon as his head hit the pillow.

As eager as Jonas was to get back on the trail again, he had to remain in Anson City to tie up loose ends. The money he'd recovered belonged to a local rancher, Matt Formosa, who had picked it up from the bank to meet his monthly payroll. The thief was a drifting cowboy named Sly Fields, who had only been in Formosa's employ for two months. He'd lain in wait for Fields to return, then knocked the rancher out with a pistol barrel to his head. Fields was overjoyed when Jonas returned the cash.

Three says after arriving at Anson City, Jonas was able to resume his journey to Sweetwater.

"We've got to cover some miles, Rebel," he told his horse, once the mustang had warmed up. "At this rate, Will's liable to reach Sweetwater before we do. I sure hope he's comin' along all right."

Rebel was eager to run after three days in a stall. Jonas let the mustang stretch his legs, allowing him to gallop for a mile, before pulling him down to a steady, mile eating lope. It was about forty-five miles from Anson City to Sweetwater. With a fresh horse between his legs, Jonas would cover the distance in one, albeit long, day.

12

Jonas reached Sweetwater shortly after ten that night. He headed straight for the building which served as the Ranger post.

"We're home, Rebel," he said to his leg weary horse. "Unless something needs immediate attention, I'm just gonna take a couple of days to catch up on paperwork and follow up on any messages that came in while we were gone. That means you'll have some time to take it easy. First thing tomorrow I'll send a telegram to Quitaque to see how Will is comin' along. Then I'll get some breakfast. After that I'm gonna head over to the barber shop for a haircut, shave, and nice long, hot bath. I'll stop by the general store to pick up some supplies for me, then the feed store to order some hay and grain delivered for you. I'll also need to stop to see the city marshal and county sheriff. Instead of riding, I'll let you stay here and rest. How's that sound?"

Rebel whickered, and tossed his head.

Jonas laughed. He slapped Rebel fondly on his neck.

"I knew that would sound mighty good to you. Well, here we are."

Jonas rode around to the back of the building and reined up. He swung out of the saddle, and led Rebel into the corral. One end of the enclosure had an opened faced shed for shelter, as well as a smaller, enclosed shed which held hay, grain, and gear. A water pump with a bucket hanging from it was alongside that. He tossed the reins over the mustang's neck. Rebel followed him across the corral. When they reached the shed, Jonas pulled his gear off Rebel. He hung the saddle, bridle, and blanket on the top rail of the corral, so they could dry out in the evening breeze. He pumped the bucket brim full, and set it down inside the corral. Rebel eagerly slurped down half the contents.

Jonas unlocked the shed, half filled another bucket with grain, and set that out. He opened a bale of hay and pulled out three flakes, which he placed next to the grain. While Rebel ate, Jonas gave him a thorough grooming.

"You're all set for tonight, pardner," he told Rebel, giving his bay one final swipe of the currycomb. "Tomorrow I'll rub you down again. I'll pull all those damn burrs out of your mane and tail."

Rebel lifted his head, snorted, and went back to munching his hay.

"I guess that's good night," Jonas said, chuckling. "Fill your belly, then go to sleep. I'll see you in the morning."

Jonas made a stop at the outhouse, then went inside, found the coal oil lamp on the front desk, lit it, and set it back down. He took a quick look around the building's single room. It was dusty after weeks of being empty; however, everything seemed to be in place. He pulled down the shades so he wouldn't be disturbed.

Jonas went over to the sink, pumped a basin full of water, along with a tin mug. He took off his hat and bandanna, splashed water on his face and hair, then used his bandanna to wipe dry. He downed the mug of water, left it in the wooden sink, then went over to the nearest bunk, which was his. He took off his gun belt and hung it from a peg over the bed, then sat down on the edge of his mattress. He removed his boots and socks, left them alongside the bunk, then stretched out on his back, looking up at the ceiling. He sighed. It was good to be back home. If only Will were here with him. Well, he'd be at Western Union as soon as their office opened. With any luck at all, there'd be a telegram from Will waiting for him. If not, he'd get his own wire right off to Quitaque to see how much longer Will would be confined to bed. With that thought on his mind, he drifted off to sleep.

The next morning, after feeding and watering Rebel, Jonas set out on his errands. Bill Thompson, the Western Union telegrapher, pushed back his green eyeshade and exclaimed in surprise when Jonas walked into the office.

"Ranger Peterson. We weren't expectin' you

back so soon. Good morning. How've you been?"

"Howdy, Bill. I'm fine. I'd planned on reaching town a few days ago, but got sidetracked. Had to swing by Anson City first. Do you have any messages for me?"

"Just one, from Ranger Kirkpatrick. Let me get it for you."

Thompson reached into a cubbyhole behind his desk, pulled out a yellow flimsy, and handed it to Jonas, who quickly scanned it.

En route to Sweetwater STOP Wait there until I arrive STOP WK STOP

"Good news?" Thompson asked.

"It damn for certain is. Will's on his way back. I didn't expect him to leave Quitaque for another few days. He was shot fightin' a bunch of bank robbers and killers. He only got it in his arm, but the bullet severed an artery, so he nearly bled to death. The doc up there wouldn't release him until he got some strength back."

"Then that is good news. You need to send any messages this morning?"

"Yeah, I need to get a couple off, one to Austin, and another to Jones County."

Thompson handed the Ranger two forms and a pencil. Jonas sat down and composed two messages. One was to Ranger Headquarters, detailing everything which had happened, promising a full report to follow by mail. The other was to the Jones County Board of Commissioners, officially notifying them that he had appointed Tom Carlson as a Special Texas Ranger and the chief law enforcement officer for Jones County, until a permanent replacement for the previous sheriff, Zeke Talbot, could be appointed. Once he was finished, he handed the forms to Thompson.

"Is there a rush on these, or can they go out after the other messages that I have waiting to be sent?"

"There's no rush."

"Then that'll be thirty-two cents."

"All right."

Jonas handed the telegrapher the required amount, plus a nickel for a tip.

"Thanks, Ranger. You can stop by later today for confirmation your messages were sent out and received."

"That'll be fine, Bill. Right now I'm goin' for some breakfast, then a haircut, shave, and bath. I should probably clean up first, but my belly's complainin' it's been far too long since I slid any decent grub down my gullet."

Thompson laughed.

"I can sure understand that. I'll see you later."

"Later."

Thomson pulled down his eyeshade, and returned his attention to his telegraph key, clickety-clacking out the dots and dashes of Morse Code that would be translated back into English by their recipients.

Jonas next went to the adjacent Timoleon's Restaurant. The owners, Greek-Americans Timoleon Chakolas and his wife Kiki, greeted him warmly when he walked in and sat down at the counter. Kiki immediately poured him a cup of steaming hot, strong coffee.

"Howdy, Jonas. It's about time you returned," she said. "Where's your partner?"

"Will's on his way from Quitaque," Jonas answered. "We had to split up for a while. He'll be here in a few days."

Jonas let it go at that. He didn't have time for a long explanation, nor the need to repeat it at every stop he made. Word about what had happened to Will would be all over town before the day was out anyway. Bill Thompson would start telling the story, and once Jonas had given the news to the marshal and sheriff it would spread like wildfire.

"What would you like for breakfast?" Kiki asked.

"Four eggs, over easy, a double order of crispy bacon, another double order of ham fried crispy, and plenty of fried potatoes, also crispy. Half a dozen biscuits and gravy. You might as well just leave the coffee pot, too."

"You must be awful hungry," Timoleon observed.

"Too many days of eating my own cookin',"

Jonas explained. "A few more days of that and I'd have died from food poisoning, or quit eating altogether and starved myself to death."

"We'll have your breakfast ready in a jiffy," Kiki assured him.

Jonas took an hour to eat his meal. Once he was finished with breakfast, he walked across the street to Antoine's Tonsorial Parlor. The owner, Antoine Bilodeaux, was a transplanted Cajun from Baton Rouge, Louisiana. It took the barber almost an hour to cut Jonas's overgrown blonde hair short, and completely remove his thick, tangled sandy beard. Once the trimming was done, Jonas headed to the back room, where he settled into a deep zinc tub of almost scalding hot water. He soaked for a good while, allowing the water to soothe his aches, and remove some of the grime from the trail. He then scrubbed himself, toweled off, and dressed in the clean clothes he had brought from the post. He dropped his dirty duds off at Wong's Chinese Laundry on his way to the Nolan County Sheriff's Office and Nolan County Courthouse. Sweetwater's City Marshal, Isaiah Melton, was just dismounting from his grulla gelding when Will walked up.

"Good mornin', Isaiah," Jonas called to him. The marshal turned and stared at him for a moment, not quite certain it was indeed Jonas.

"Ranger Peterson. If you ain't a sight for sore

eyes. Where the devil have you been? And where in blue blazes is Will? And why the hell are you on foot? What happened to your horse?"

"Will should be along in a few days," Jonas answered. "We ran into a bit of trouble up around Quitaque. I'll give you the entire tale at the same time I tell the sheriff. No use in repeatin' the same story twice. I'm walking because Rebel needed a good rest."

Melton looped his grulla's reins over the rail. He stroked his horse's neck.

"You just stay here and relax, Pedro. I'm gonna be awhile. C'mon, Jonas, let's head inside. I've got a meeting with the sheriff myself. There's a lot you need to know, none of it good."

They went inside the building and straight to Sheriff Roy Hamilton's office. The sheriff was reading a two day old newspaper. He set it aside and blinked when he saw Jonas with Melton. Hamilton was in his late forties, with wavy black hair, deep brown eyes, and skin tanned the color of deep brown leather by years of exposure to the harsh Texas Panhandle sun and wind. He stood around five foot eight, and weighed a wiry one hundred and fifty pounds. Despite his age, he had no fat around his middle. Every one of those hundred and fifty pounds was muscle and bone. The veteran lawman was not one to be trifled with.

"Jonas! I didn't expect to see you this morning. Where's Will?"

"Still up in Quitaque, but he should be heading back now. We had a rough trip."

"Pour yourself a cup of coffee, light up a smoke, and tell me all about it."

"Isaiah informed me you've got some real trouble around here, too."

"We damn sure do. Your story will be shorter, I'm certain. So you go first."

"I'm not so sure about that. But I'll be as brief as I can. There'll be enough time to fill in the details later."

Jonas and Isaiah both took mugs from a shelf, and poured them full of coffee from the pot kept simmering on the stove. They sat down, rolled and lit quirlies. Hamilton relit the half-smoked cigar he had clenched between his teeth. The cheroot's butt was chewed almost through.

"Speak your piece, Jonas."

"Four men robbed the bank up in Quitaque. They gunned down several people. Will and I tailed them down into Crawfish Canyon. We thought we had the *hombres* cornered. We were wrong. They had laid a trap, and we rode right into it. Will got shot right off. He was only hit in his arm, and the wound didn't seem too bad, but he soon lost consciousness. I was lucky enough to take care of those bastards. They're all buried in the Quitaque Cemetery."

"What about Will?" Melton asked.

"I'm comin' to that. It turned out the bullet he

took nicked an artery. He nearly bled out before I got him back to town. Quitaque's doctor is a really fine *medico*. He was able to fix Will up and pull him through. But he had to stay behind and rest up. There was a wire waitin' for me at the telegraph office this morning from him, sayin' he was on his way back."

"I hope he doesn't take too long," Hamilton said. "Begging your pardon, Jonas, but you look like you've been through more than just that. More like Hell and back."

"I have. Quick list. While me'n Will were on the trail of the holdup men, a rich rancher's son murdered a wrangler in Quitaque. The usual causes, liquor and a woman. When one of the county deputies went out to the ranch to arrest him, the family drove him off. He was wounded in the attempt. Me'n him were goin' back after the suspect, but the family attacked the jail before we could. More dead, including the rancher and two of his sons. Then I got caught in a wicked storm that held me up. Also had some son of a bitch try'n steal my horse. I had to kill him. Turned out he had robbed the Anson City bank. So I had to swing by there. I found out the Frank Wilson gang had made the town their headquarters. They'd killed three lawmen, and driven the county sheriff out of town. So me and the only deputy left, an old man, who has more sand in his craw than a lot of younger ones, tangled with the outfit. They're all six feet under. After that, I rode straight here. Now it's your turn, Roy."

"Well, I have to say I was wrong at least in one way. You've been through a helluva lot more bad situations than we've been. However, we've got one that tops all yours put together."

Jonas let out a grim laugh. He shook his head.

"I don't know if I should even ask what you mean."

"We've got the usual troubles, of course. Cowboys comin' to town, gettin' drunk, and raisin' a ruckus. A night in a cell usually cools then off, although sometimes they need a gun barrel bent over their thick skulls to convince 'em to come along peaceably. Cattle rustlin' and horse thieving. Neighbors feuding with each other, and of course thefts."

"But there's more."

"There damn sure is. You know there'd been a rash of stage holdups over Abilene way. A few weeks ago, there was another stagecoach robbery, of the Dallas to Albuquerque stage, only about thirty miles east of here. It took place between Merkel and Trent, over in Taylor County. The perpetrators killed everyone on board, took all the valuables and the strongbox, but for some reason left the stagecoach and horses. Then the stage that runs from here down to San Angelo was hit. That was the first one in Nolan County. Since then, there's been five more holdups, all over this section, from Abilene clear west to Big Spring. Every damn one's been pulled the same way. The gang waits for the stage, waylays it, kills the driver, shotgun guard, and all the passengers, but leaves the stage and the horses. No, to answer your question, they don't shoot the horses. Kind of strange, I know. From what we've been able to piece together, it looks like a half dozen men in the outfit. Whoever they are, they don't want to leave any witnesses behind. The worst one was a couple of weeks ago, when they hit the Dallas to Albuquerque stage. Two of the passengers were a young married couple from back East. It appears the husband shot his wife to keep the gang from having their way with her, then he killed himself."

Hamilton paused to shake his head.

"Damn shame."

"You haven't had any luck picking up their trail?" Jonas asked.

The sheriff shook his head again.

"None at all. No one has. They're real good at hiding their tracks. And they're smart bastards, too. There's no pattern to the holdups. You never know where they're going to pop up next. You can't go by whatever any particular stage might be carrying, neither. They've hit short line coaches with only a few passengers and no strongbox, to that Dallas—Albuquerque stage, which was their biggest haul, at least so far. Ten thousand dollars in brand new gold double eagles headed to the Albuquerque banks. Plus whatever valuables they took from the mail sack, and off the dead folks."

"Do you have reports on each robbery, even the ones that weren't in Nolan County?"

"Right here in my file cabinet."

"You mind if I take them back to the post with me? I'd like to spend the rest of the day goin' through them."

"I don't mind, but why not just read then right here?" Hamilton asked.

"I want to read them by myself first," Jonas answered. "That way I won't be interrupted. I'll write down any questions I have, and ask you those when I return the files."

"You reckon that'll be tonight?"

"No. Not until morning. I've still got to get supplies for the post, and order feed for my horse. I also like to sleep on something after I read it. Sometimes a person might wake up from a sound sleep with an idea that comes to him in the middle of the night. I keep a piece of paper and a pencil next to my bed, in case that happens. It's a trick I learned from Will."

"All right. I know they're safe in your hands," Hamilton said. "With any luck you'll be back tomorrow with the good news you found something in these files that might've been overlooked."

Hamilton went to the file cabinet, opened it, removed a stack of thick manila folders and handed them to Jonas.

"Looks like I've got my work cut out for me," Jonas said. "Good thing I don't have to wear spectacles to read. I'll get these back to you as quick as I can."

"Take all the time you need. The law all around these parts is stumped, so those files are useless as far as I'm concerned."

"I'm obliged, Sheriff. Might as well finish up my other business and get to work on these. Lemme get goin'."

"I'll catch up with you later, Ranger," Melton said. "I've got to be in court in about twenty minutes. Have to testify in an assault case."

"I've also got to testify in the same case," Hamilton added.

"Good enough. If either of you happen to think of anything at all that might help me, once I make my stops, I'll be at the post until tomorrow morning. I'll swing by then and drop off these files. See you *mañana*."

"See you tomorrow," Hamilton said.

It took Jonas about an hour to order feed for his horse to be delivered, and stop by the Sweetwater Mercantile to get needed supplies for the post's larder, along with gun cleaning supplies and more ammunition. He also purchased two new pairs of socks. Once he was done, he went back to the post, fed and watered Rebel, then went inside, turned up the lamp, stretched out on his bed, and opened the first file.

It's gonna take most of the night to plow through all this. Good thing I bought more Arbuckle's. I'll drink a lot of coffee before this day is done.

13

While Jonas was starting to investigate the stagecoach robberies, Will was working his way southward toward Sweetwater. Finally disgusted with lying in bed, he defied Doctor Lynch's orders and left four days ahead of schedule.

Will knew he should take it easy on the journey; however, he needed to get some of the knots out of his muscles, while Pete was rested and eager to run. He let the overo set his own pace. Pete started out with a few bucks, then went into a gallop for over a mile, before settling down to a ground covering lope. He would slow to a jogtrot or walk for a while, then resume the lope. With only a few short breaks to give both himself and his horse breathers, and a quick bite to eat with a short drink of water, Will was approaching Roaring Springs well before sundown.

"All right, Pete, we're gonna stop for the night, soon as we reach the Springs," Will said, patting his horse on the shoulder. "Neither one of us should chance overdoin' it the first day out. We'll get a good rest, then start out at dawn tomorrow."

Pete snorted and shook his head. After days of confinement, the paint wanted to keep on moving.

"Don't forget who's boss, and who feeds you

those treats, you old pie-biter," Will said with a laugh, and a fond slap to Pete's neck. "I've had enough for today, and you'll be glad we stopped, too. Plenty of grass and cool, sweet water at Roaring Springs for you."

Once they reached their destination for the night, Will, like all good horsemen, tended to his horse's needs before his own. He stripped the gear from Pete and gave him a good grooming, then turned him loose to drink and graze.

"Time to have my own supper. At least I don't have to cook tonight."

Sarah Lynch had provided Will enough thick ham and cheese sandwiches, pickles, biscuits, hard boiled eggs, and freshly baked oatmeal cookies to provide Will with breakfast and supper for the first two days of his trip. He removed two sandwiches and three cookies from his saddlebags. Foregoing his usual coffee, he filled his tin mug with water from the spring, then sat down on a nearby log to enjoy his meal.

As soon as he was done eating, Will checked on Pete one last time, then had a final cigarette before rolling out his blankets and turning in. The night was cool and clear, the stars so bright it seemed he could almost reach up and touch them. He spent some time lost in thought.

Why do I keep doin' this, being away from home for weeks at a time, riskin' my life chasin' lawbreakers all over Texas? One of these days my luck's gonna run out, and an outlaw's bullet will take my life. I could become a town marshal or county deputy just as easy, and be home every night, mebbe find a nice girl to settle down with. I must be plumb loco.

A sudden meteor shower, with dozens of shooting stars flashing across the night sky, provided the answer which Will already knew. He never could stay in one place for long, loved being a Texas Ranger, and would be one until he could no longer ride for days, or until a renegade's bullet cut his life short.

Content, Will drifted off to sleep. Unlike Jonas at the same spot a few days previously, he slept unmolested until dawn.

Will covered even more miles the next day. Pete showed no signs of flagging, so once again the sturdy paint set a fast pace. Will decided to spend the night in Jay Flat, almost fifty miles south of where he had begun the day.

Jay Flat was a small settlement, named after a local ranching family. In future years, its name would be changed to Jayton, and in 1954, after a long and bitter court battle, Jayton would become the seat of Kent County, taking that title away from the nearby dying town of Clairemont, which would soon become a virtual ghost town. Jay Flat's economy was supported mainly by cattle ranching and cotton farming. The discovery of oil saved Jayton from falling victim to the Great Depression and Dust Bowl years of the 1930s, sparing it the fate of so many small farming towns of the southern Great Plains. While the agricultural industries were devastated during those grim years, oil kept the town alive.

Will rode down Jay Flat's single street about four in the afternoon. Because he looked like any of a thousand other drifting, chuck-line-riding saddle tramp cowboys, no one paid much attention to him. Since most cowboys disdained riding paint horses, deriding them as "Indian ponies," Pete might have aroused some curiosity, but the chunky, close coupled gelding's appearance was so nondescript even he didn't catch anyone's eye. He looked like a horse any down on his luck cowhand might ride, the only one he could afford. That ordinary look belied the horse's courage, speed, and stamina.

"Looks like the livery stable just ahead, Pete," Will told his horse. "You'll be munching down oats in no time."

A few moments later, Will was dismounting in front of the Jay Flat Livery Stable. Having seen him approach, a tow-haired young man of about nineteen got up from the empty horseshoe keg on which he was sitting. He was chewing on a blade of hay.

"Howdy, Mister. I'm Jeb Dailey, the stable owner. Lookin' for a stall for your horse?"

"I sure am. Name's Will Kirkpatrick. This here's Pete. Double ration of oats, plenty of hay and water, and a good rubdown, too. We covered a lot of miles the past two days, and we've got to be in Sweetwater by tomorrow night."

"That's still a good distance off. Where'd you start from?"

"Quitaque."

"Quitaque? No wonder you both look so tired. All the horses in my care get nothing but the best. I'll take good care of Pete for you."

He stroked Pete's nose. Will's horse nickered.

"We're gonna get along just fine, aren't we, Pete, ol' feller?"

Pete tossed his head.

"It's fifty cents for the stall, feed, and rubdown. Another dime for the extra oats, Mister. Is that all right?"

"It's more than fair. But the name's Will, not Mister."

"Understood."

Will dug a silver dollar out of his pocket.

"Here ya go. The change is yours."

"Gee, thanks, Will. Thanks a heap."

"*Por nada.* Where can I get a room for the night, and a decent meal?"

"Jay Flat's too small for a hotel. Mrs. Brannigan's boarding house is seven buildings down, on this side of the road. It's a two-story house painted white with blue trim. She keeps the place clean, and serves up a real tasty supper and breakfast. Or you can sleep here in the hayloft."

"I've done that plenty of times, Jeb, but Mrs. Brannigan's place sounds like it'll be a lot more comfortable, especially after two long days in the saddle. I'll head on over there."

"That's what I'd do. What time will you want your horse ready? Mrs. Brannigan serves breakfast at seven. Not a minute sooner, not a minute later. Supper's at five, again, not a minute sooner, not a minute later. You'll need to hurry if you want to eat tonight."

"I'd hoped to get an earlier start, like at sunup, but you're right about both me'n Pete being bone tired. I'll pick him up right after breakfast."

"I'll have him fed, watered, saddled, and ready to hit the trail. See you *mañana*."

"*Mañana.*"

Jonas picked up his rifle, shouldered his saddlebags, and made the short walk to Mrs. Brannigan's boarding house. The place was easy enough to find, with colorful flowers of many varieties blooming in the yard and in clay pots at the front door. A small sign next to the door read "Rooms to Let."

Jonas knocked on the door. It was soon answered by a sixtyish, gray haired, auburn eyed plump woman, about five feet six inches tall, dressed in a blue cotton dress over which was a flour dusted white apron. Her hair was pulled back in a tight bun, her face flushed from the heat of the kitchen. She held a dishtowel.

"Yeah, Mister? What can I do for you?"

"My name's Will Kirkpatrick. Jeb Dailey at the livery stable recommended you as having clean rooms to rent, Ma'am. I need a place to stay for the night."

The woman looked Jonas up and down.

"The name's Dorothy Brannigan. Room's a dollar a night, includes supper and breakfast, paid in advance. Supper's at five, breakfast's at seven. I don't make any early meals, so don't ask. If you're not at the table when I put out the food, you go hungry. If you want a bath I've got a tub out back. Curtain around it for privacy. You fill it yourself, and make certain you drain it when you're done. Twenty-five cents for a cold bath, fifty cents if you want hot water. Either one gets you a towel and soap. I don't put up with any nonsense, noise, or smoking inside. You can go out to the saloon, but come back drunk and you won't be allowed back in my house. Understand all that?"

"Yes, Mrs. Brannigan, I sure do. I'm not looking for anything but a bed to sleep in and a good meal. Although I will take you up on the bath. The night's a mite sticky, so cold will be just fine."

"You'll have to take it after supper, or you'll miss the meal. I have three other guests right now. Follow me and I'll show you the room."

She led Will through the parlor, kitchen, and down a long, wainscoted corridor, painted a seafoam green, decorated with floral still lifes hanging on the walls. She opened the third door on the left.

"Wait here while I light the lamp."

She went into the room, lit the coal oil lamp on the nightstand, and adjusted the flame.

"C'mon in and have a looksee."

Will walked into a lemon-yellow painted room, just large enough to hold a bed, small bureau, nightstand, and straight-backed chair. There was a plump pillow at the head of the bed, which was covered with white sheets and a hand-crocheted bedspread. A pitcher, basin, bar of soap, and a towel were on the bureau, and ceramic chamber pot under the bed.

"Is this satisfactory, Mr. Kirkpatrick?"

"It's better than most hotels I've stayed at. I'll take it."

Will took a silver dollar and a fifty-cent piece from his pocket and handed them to the landlady.

"I thought you said a cold bath?"

"I did. The extra twenty-five cents is for you."

"Well, thank you. Supper's in ten minutes. That should give you just enough time to clean up. Your key is on the nightstand. If you decide to step out after supper, I lock the outside doors at eleven. Be back by then."

"I will," Will assured her.

Mrs. Brannigan left, closing the door behind her. Will poured some water into the basin. He washed his hands and face, then dried off.

"That's all I've got the time for, if I want my supper. And I sure do. I'm plumb starved."

When Will reached the kitchen, the other three boarders were already at the table. He took one of the remaining chairs. The others introduced themselves as Thomas Hardy, a traveling book salesman, Ezekiel Hollingsworth, who owned the small general store and made the boarding house his home, and Abraham Joiner, a circuit riding Methodist preacher. Will introduced himself as a horse wrangler on his way to a new job at a ranch outside Sweetwater. He wouldn't reveal his true identity as a Texas Ranger unless it became necessary. Joiner led everyone in a brief Grace before they tucked into a meal of beef stew, fresh from the oven crusty bread, coffee, and a cherry pie for dessert. Will found the meal delicious, the company and conversation pleasant. In exactly one hour, Mrs. Brannigan ordered everyone out of the kitchen. Hardy and Hollingsworth went to the parlor for a friendly game of cards. Joiner retired to his room to read Scripture passages from his Bible. Will decided to take his bath before heading over to Jay Flat's only saloon, to have a couple of beers before calling it a night.

• • •

Befitting its location in the small settlement, the Jay Flat Saloon was smaller than most. There was a short bar at the rear of the room, as usual backed by a mirror. There were two card tables, but no places for other games such as faro or chuck-a-luck. There was no beat up, out of tune piano, no dance floor, and not a percentage girl in sight. Contrary to popular belief, most small-town saloons in the West were just that, drinking establishments, with a card table or two. Gambling, dancing, and more unsavory pursuits generally were in their own establishments, in the larger towns and big cities. Small town saloons were for ranchers, workers, and local business owners to gather for drinks and friendly conversations. Arguments might happen, but physical fights rare, gunfights ever more so.

The saloon's owner greeted Will warmly.

"Howdy, stranger. C'mon in. My name's Eli Hunter. I own this little ol' place, such as it is."

Will found an empty space between two cowboys and bellied up to the bar.

"Will Kirkpatrick. Just passing through on my way to Sweetwater. Stopped for the night. The liveryman told me best place in town for overnight guests was Mrs. Brannigan's, so that's where I'm stayin'."

"Then welcome to Jay Flat. If you meet with Dottie's approval then you must be an all right fella. She's a good judge of character. What'll you have? First one's on the house."

"Beer."

"One beer comin' right up."

Hardy drew a mug of beer and set in in front of Will, who sampled it, then smiled.

"Real good beer."

"Why, thank you, kind sir. Let me introduce these other men to you."

Will spent the next two hours sipping beer and talking with the six other patrons in the bar. He drained his last mug, then bade good night to the others.

Will had almost reached the front door when the batwings swung in. A young cowboy, no more than seventeen or eighteen years old, stumbled through them. He staggered into Will. The smell of whiskey was strong on the young man's breath.

"Watch where you're goin', ya damn fool idjit," the cowboy cursed, slurring his words.

"Sorry," Will answered, wanting to avoid trouble, even though he knew the man had bumped into him.

"Sorry ain't good enough, Mister. You scuffed my new boots, and like to broke my damn foot. You're gonna have to pay for that."

The cowboy backed up about three paces, his green eyes glaring at Will. His hand hovered over the Remington .44 hanging at his right hip.

"Jamie Slayton, didn't I tell you to go home and sleep off all the whiskey you guzzled tonight?" Hunter yelled. "So get outta here. You know I don't allow any trouble in my place. Now go on home. Git!"

"Not without another bottle of whiskey to take with me. After I kill this here *hombre*. No one tangles with Jamie Johnston Slayton and gets away with it. Mister, you'd better go for your gun. I'm gonna kill you right where you stand if you don't. 'Course, you're about to die anyway. I'm the fastest gun in these parts. Mebbe all of Texas. Mebbe even the whole damn Yew-Nighted States of America. Mexico and Canada too. Don't think of turning yeller and tryin' to make a run for it, neither. No one makes a fool of me."

"They don't have to," Will said, his voice low and menacing. "You appear to be doin' a fine job of that all by yourself. You don't need help from anyone else. Take Mr. Hunter's advice and go home. You're just a kid who's had way too much to drink. Listen to me before things go too far, and you can't stop what happens. You can't put a bullet back in a gun once the trigger's been pulled."

"I'm done talkin'. Go for your gun."

Slayton's hand dove for his six-gun. He froze with the hand wrapped around the gun's butt, the Remington still in its holster.

Will had already pulled his gun and held it leveled at the young cowboy's stomach. Slayton's eyes grew wide with shock and fear. Looking into the muzzle of Will's long-barreled Colt Peacemaker, he saw .45 caliber death ready to snuff out his life. He began trembling. Will walked up to Slayton, pulled his gun from its holster, emptied the bullets and put them in his own pocket, tossed the Remington onto the bar, then shoved Slayton in the chest, sending him stumbling backwards across the room until he tripped and landed on his butt on the floor. Will grabbed Slayton's shirtfront, pulled him to his feet, and pushed him against the wall, still holding onto the shirt. He slapped the young cowboy twice across the face.

"Listen here, and listen close, you damn, stupid fool. You're lucky it was me you picked on tonight, kid. Almost any other man would have put a bullet through your guts and been done with it. You'd've been left lying in a puddle of your own blood soaking into the sawdust on this here saloon's floor. Then someone would have had to tell your ma and pa you'd been gunned down because you were drunk, and thought you were real fast with a gun. How do you think that would have hit them? They'd never get over knowin' their son was gunned down in a meaningless gun fight in a saloon, just because he was tryin' to prove how big a man he was. And if you have any sisters or brothers, what about them? Or your other kinfolk. Lemme tell you somethin'. No matter how fast you are, or think you are, there's always someone faster. You might win a few gun duels, but sooner or later that faster man'll come along and kill you. Either that, or you'll get arrested and hung for murder first. Is that what you want? Because that's what's gonna happen if you keep travelin' down the road you're on. You act like you're tough, and quick on the draw. Hell, you ain't even old enough to grow a decent beard yet. Nothin' but peach fuzz whiskers on your face. And I just showed you you're not fast at all. Are you fixin' to try'n challenge another man who comes along to a showdown? Because next time that *hombre*'ll beat you to the draw, just like I did. Only that man won't hesitate to pull the trigger. Is that how you want to die?"

Tears flowed from Slayton's eyes, whether of fear, shame, relief, or a combination of all three Will couldn't tell.

"No. No. Just lemme go, Mister."

"Not until I'm certain you've learned your lesson."

Will let go of the boy's shirt, pulled his badge out of his pocket and pinned it to his vest.

"I'm a Texas Ranger. You had no way of knowin' that, nor of knowin' whomever you might be messin' with when you pull your gun on somebody, or challenge 'em to a showdown. For all you knew, I could've been a cold-blooded killer on the run. You think a man like that would show you any mercy? Cut you any slack?"

"N . . . No."

"You're damn right he wouldn't. I could arrest you for breach of peace, at the very least. This town got a jail, Eli?"

Hunter shook his head.

"Nope. Hell, we're still part of Fisher County. The state's supposed to organize a new county, breaking us off from Fisher County, but it ain't even been mapped out yet. There's talk about it, but so far nothin's happened. We rely on the county sheriff, but he's way down in Roby. We don't usually have much trouble around here in any event. We can handle most of it without needing the law involved."

"Son, your good fortune keeps on goin'," Will said. "I don't have the time to haul you all the way to Roby. I'll be passin' through there, but I'll be ridin' fast. I can't waste time waitin' for you to sober up and be fit enough to travel. Where's your home?"

"My folks have a small ranch about six miles north of town,"

"I'm headed south, or I'd take you home myself, and let them deal with you," Will said. "So you head out there right now. I will stop at the sheriff's office in Roby, leave him a report, and make certain he checks up on you. You're too young to throw your life away on such foolishness as you showed here tonight. So go on home, and help your folks with that ranch. When the time comes, find yourself a nice gal, settle down and get married. You understand?"

"Yessir, Ranger. I purely do. Can I have my gun back?"

"I'll leave it with Eli. You can have it back in a week, after you've come to your senses. And if you're thinkin' about not lettin' your folks know about what happened here tonight, forget about that. Eli, you got a piece of paper and a pencil?"

"I sure do, Ranger."

"Good. Jamie, I'm gonna write up a letter and have Eli get it to your folks. You don't seem like that bad a young man. Just have some growing up to do. But if you keep hittin' the whiskey bottle and challenging strangers with your gun, you'll never have the chance. I've got a partner who started out on the wrong side of the law, but he got straightened out. Now he's a Texas Ranger. If you want to take a lawman's job, think about joinin' up with the Rangers, where you can do a lot of good. Or mebbe Jayton'll grow large enough to hire you on as a town marshal. You've got a lot of choices ahead of you. Don't make the wrong one."

Slayton was scared half sober after his close call.

"I won't, Ranger. I promise you that."

"I'm takin' your word. I'll be back this way

some day, and I'll stop by to see how you're doin'. Now go on home. And don't fall off your horse and break your dang neck."

"I won't."

Slayton scrambled out the door. It took him three tries to get into his saddle, but he did, and the shuffling hoof beats of his horse heading out of town at a slow walk indicated he was headed for home.

"Eli, I didn't mean to put you on the spot," Will said, as he took the bullets from Slayton's gun out of his pocket and handed them to the saloon keeper. "You don't have to get the letter to that boy's folks for me."

"Don't apologize, Ranger. I want to do you that little favor. As you said, Jamie's not a bad kid, just kind of wild, like so many young'ns his age. What happened here tonight was just what he needed."

"Then I'm obliged. And I'd better hurry and get it written so I can get back to Mrs. Brannigan's before she locks me out."

"Which she will. Her doors are locked at eleven on the dot, come Hell or high water. I'm gonna close up for the night now anyway. The rest of you gents, finish your drinks and go on home to your wives and children."

14

Will knew, having to cover more than sixty miles, he wouldn't reach Sweetwater until after dark in any event, at least not without killing his horse, so he kept Pete at a steady pace, alternating between a trot and a slow lope, with plenty of stretches where he allowed the overo to walk. It was after nine o'clock when he rode into Sweetwater. Not wanting anything but rest for both his horse and himself, he stuck to the shadows, allowing the dark to cloak him so he wouldn't be recognized and stopped. When he reached the Ranger post, he went around back to put up his horse for the night.

Rebel was in the corral. He whinnied a noisy greeting when he saw Pete, his buddy and traveling partner.

"Shh, Rebel," Will told the mustang. "I didn't see any light on, so Jonas must be asleep. Let's not wake him up, all right?"

Rebel nickered. He trailed along behind Will as he walked Pete across the corral, knowing when Will's horse got fed, he'd at least get some hay to munch on.

Will led Pete into the horse shed, where he removed his gear. The horse shook, glad to be relieved of the weight.

"I reckon that must feel good, eh, boy?"

Will slapped Pete on the shoulder. He took his saddle, saddle blanket, and bridle to the feed shed, where he half-filled one bucket with grain, put a half quart of oats in a second to keep Rebel busy, along with good sized servings of hay for each horse. After filling the water bucket, he set the grain and hay down for each horse, then rubbed down Pete and cleaned out his hooves.

"I know you're as tuckered out as I am, old pard, so you finish your supper and go to sleep. We'll take tomorrow off, well, you will, anyway. If nothing else, I've got plenty of paperwork to get done. G'night, horse."

Pete lifted his head, nickered, then went back to chewing on his hay. Will shouldered his saddlebags, took the door key from his vest pocket, picked up his Winchester and headed inside.

"That you, Will?" Jonas murmured from his bunk, his voice heavy with sleep.

"You'd damn well better hope it is, not some skulkin' ambusher," Will answered. "Yeah, it's me. I was hoping to come in without wakin' you up."

"You didn't. Rebel did. When I heard him neighin' his fool head off, I knew it had to be you come home. You doin' all right?"

"I am. You?"

"I'm just fine. But we've got a lot to talk about."

"Anything that can't wait until morning?"
"Nope."
"Good. I'm gonna get me some much needed sleep."

Will dropped his saddlebags onto the chair next to his bed, and placed his rifle on the floor alongside it. He didn't even bother to remove his boots, just crashed face down on his bed. He never even felt his head hit the pillow.

15

Will was awakened the next morning by the delicious aromas and mouth-watering sounds of bacon and eggs sizzling in the pan, biscuits rising, and coffee boiling in the pot. He stretched and let out a huge yawn.

Jonas turned away from the stove and grinned at Will.

"It's about time you woke up, old man. I thought perhaps you'd died in your sleep. Of course, I wasn't worried. My cookin's good enough to bring a dead man back to life. You hungry? The food's just about ready."

"Sayin' I'm hungry is puttin' it mildly, Jonas. I'm plumb starved. Even hungry enough to chow down some of your lousy grub, despite your high opinion of your culinary talents, which are sorely lacking. And exactly whom do you think you're callin' old?"

"Hey, if you can call me fat, like you did back in Crawfish Canyon, then I figure I can call you old," Jonas retorted.

"I wouldn't count on it," Will shot back. "I'd better hit the outhouse and wash up a bit before I eat. Horses fed?"

"They are. Breakfast will be on the table by the

time you're done with your chore. Unless you're feelin' all stopped up."

Will shook his head. He got out of bed and scratched his belly, then ran a hand through his hair. He emitted a long and loud belch.

"If anything, it's the opposite. I'd better make a run for it."

Will hustled out the back door, with Jonas's laughter ringing in his ears.

Once Will returned and washed up, the two Rangers sat down to their breakfast.

"Did you have any trouble on the way home?" Jonas asked.

Will chewed the forkful of eggs in his mouth and washed them down with a swallow of coffee before he answered. He shook his head.

"Not really. Just a young kid up in Jay Flat who thought he wanted to become a famous fast draw gunfighter. I talked him out of that right quick. How about you?"

"I had a trifle more than that. I'll tell you about it while we eat. Soon as we're finished and the dishes are done, I'll catch you up to everything that's happened while we were up in Quitaque. We've got one helluva job ahead of us."

As soon as breakfast was done and the dishes washed, dried, and put away, Jonas took Will over to the room's single desk, where he had a map of the northern Texas and the Panhandle region spread out. A number of manila folders were stacked on the desk chair.

"While I was waiting for you to get here, I went through all the complaints that came in while we were gone, and organized them in order of importance," Jonas explained. "There's enough of 'em for a whole troop of Rangers, let alone just the two of us. However, there's one that stands out head and shoulders above the rest."

"The stage robberies, right?"

"You're dang tootin' the stage robberies. There were several more while we were gone. The worst one was the holdup of the Dallas to Albuquerque stage, about thirty or so miles east of here. It was a real massacre, including a young couple from back East. It appears the husband shot his wife to keep her from falling into the outlaws' clutches, then killed himself. The other holdups were almost as bad. If you want, you can read about them. The reports are in those files on the chair. But I need to go over somethin' with you first. Look here."

Jonas leaned over the map of northern Texas and the Panhandle.

"Each one of these thumbtacks marks the site of a robbery. You'll notice that every one to the east of Sweetwater took place to the east of the nearest big town. Every one to the west of Sweetwater took place to the west of the nearest town. And every one of those towns was an overnight stop. I figure the *hombres* pullin' off these holdups are right clever sons of bitches. They know the horses would be tired, so the driver wouldn't have even half a chance of outrunnin' them. The shotgun guard would be mighty weary, too. Neither he nor the driver would be as alert as earlier in the day. Plus, having gotten along so far with no trouble, and nearing town, they'd let down their guard a little. It's just human nature. That's when the robbers would hit."

"Yet no one saw anything, or anyone, suspicious?"

"Not one damn thing. The robbers must've come in from the east at the holdups before Sweetwater, the west from the ones to the west. That way they avoided any towns. It seems like they must've retraced their routes to get away. Since they killed everyone on the stages, the murders and robberies wouldn't be discovered until someone came along. And of course there would be no witnesses to identify the gang members."

"And if someone did stumble upon them in the act they'd kill them also," Will noted.

"That happened at one, the one near Big Spring. Of course, if the sons of bitches saw someone else coming before they stopped the stage, they could just call the whole thing off, and wait for another day."

"What else do you have?"

"It's gotta be the same outfit because at every holdup, the horses haven't been shot to stop the stage. Hoof prints show a half dozen men or so involved. The few tracks the local law has been able to find have almost all gone south, then most of 'em disappeared on the hardpan and caliche. But one set, from the holdup nearest Sweetwater, was goin' more southeast. And the trail from the holdup between Baird and Clyde headed west before turning southwest. But none of the trails went for more than a quarter mile before they petered out. Posses searched all around, but the tracks completely disappeared. Whoever's behind these robberies and killings are experts at covering their trail."

"You've done some fine detective work, Jonas," Will said. "From the directions of the various tracks that were found, it seems the gang holes up somewhere south of here, but it's an awful lot of ground to cover."

"I'd like to catch those bastards before they kill anyone else," Will."

"So would I. The Dallas to Albuquerque stage holdup was the one nearest to here, is that right?"

"Yeah, it is."

"Then let's ride on out there. Even after all this time, we should be able to turn up something."

"I'm with you on that, but first I'd like you to

take a looksee at the stagecoach. You might find somethin' I missed."

"It's still here?"

"Yup. Wells Fargo hasn't decided if they want to repair it or just turn it into scrap. But it's not at their depot, for obvious reasons. They wouldn't want any of their passengers to see a shot up Concord. It's stored behind the livery stable, until they make up their mind what they're gonna do with it."

"No, it damn for certain wouldn't do. Let's saddle up the horses and go take a look."

They retrieved their horses, got the gear on them, mounted, and made the short ride to the livery stable.

"The stable's got a new owner, Will. He's a real nice feller. Loves horses, so he takes real good care of 'em. Treats every one like it's a family member."

They dismounted, and dropped Pete's and Rebel's reins to the dirt to ground hitch them. They went inside the barn, and found the owner at his desk, making out invoices. He looked up when he heard them walk in.

"Ah, Ranger Peterson," he said, in heavily accented English. "It's good to see you again. I see you have a friend. Howdy, as you Texans say. My most humble apologies if I mispronounced the word."

"You did just fine, Daraj," Jonas answered.

"This is my pardner, Ranger Will Kirkpatrick. Will, Daraj Patel."

"It's an honor to meet you. Ranger Kirkpatrick," Patel said, as they shook hands. "Even in my home city of Bangalore, in my native country of India, the reputations of the Texas Rangers as courageous law officers, fearless in their pursuit of wrongdoers, is well known."

"It's a pleasure to meet you also," Will answered. "There's no need to be so formal. The name's Will."

"Excellent."

"Daraj, I brought Will over to look at the stagecoach Wells Fargo is storing here. I hope he'll be able to uncover something that I might've been missed. I'm sure hopin' so, because right now we're at a dead end."

"Of course. You know where the coach is. You left your horses outside?"

"We did," Jonas confirmed.

"I will bring them inside, and offer them water and hay while you do your work."

"That'd be much appreciated," Will said. "C'mon, Jonas, take me to the stage."

They walked through the stable and out the rear doors.

"There it is, Will."

"Boy howdy, they really shot that thing up," Will exclaimed.

"You ain't seen the half of it," Jonas said. "You

need to look around the inside, then climb up top and take a look at what's left of the baggage and roof."

Will first went inside the stage. He examined the bullets lodged in the floor and seats, the bullet holes in those and the thin wooden side panels, the holes in the roof where some of the bullets had punched through. He searched under the seats, making certain he looked into even the deepest corners, while Jonas watched form outside the coach.

"Did you find anything?" he asked, when Will stepped out of the coach.

"Just this. Take a look at it," Will said. He held out a long hank of bright red hair.

"Where'd you find that?" Jonas asked.

"Wedged in one of the seat springs. I'd wager one of the passenger yanked it off one of our suspects before she was finished off."

"She? The woman?"

"If you look close you'll see a piece of fingernail tangled in the hair. Long and polished, so it's a woman'd fingernail. We find a man with hair this color and a chink missing, it places him at the robbery."

"It also helps there's not a lot of men with hair that red," Jonas observed.

"You're right. I've also got a couple of ideas," Will answered. "I'll know more once I get on top."

Will clambered into the driver's and guard's seat, again studying several bullet holes from outlaw slugs which had passed through the unfortunate men's bodies and lodged in the front wall of the stage, splattering it with blood. He climbed onto the roof and examined the bullet holes in it and their paths through the luggage. Once finished, he dropped back to the ground.

"So tell me, Will? Any clues?"

"Yup, but not a helluva lot to help us, Jonas. This gang pullin' these holdups isn't takin' any chances. They're damn smart, too. Probably some of the smartest I've come across in my entire career as a Ranger. Time for you to learn some more investigative techniques."

"Go ahead. I'm pretty well stumped, so I'm ready to listen to everything you have to say."

"I'm just goin' from what I've seen of this stagecoach, but I'd bet my hat the others were shot up just as badly, if not worse. When we get back to the post, I'm hoping at least some of the reports on the other robberies will confirm my suspicions."

"Keep talkin'."

"Take a look at the front of the stage. You can see the bullet holes behind the driver's seat. They must've gone through both the driver and shotgun, then into the coach. The holes indicate the slugs mostly went in almost straight, not at an angle from above or below. That tells me at least two men on horseback, mebbe a couple more, lay in wait, then rode out of cover and waylaid the stage when it came into view. My guess is they started shootin' before the guard or driver even had half a chance to bring their guns into play."

"What about the passengers?"

"I'm comin' to that. You said you took a look at the top of the stage. What'd that tell you?"

"That a whole passel of *mal hombres* poured a bunch of lead into it from above. It looks like a sieve."

"Good observation. You're exactly right. My guess, actually it's more than just a guess, is the rest of the outfit was hidin' on top of a ridge or the edge of a cut made to level the grade on a steep section of road. Once the driver and guard were out of action, the men up above put enough lead into the stage to sink a good-sized ship. There was no way anyone could come out of that alive. The only thing puzzlin' me is why didn't they shoot the horses?"

"What about the young couple, the one from back East? They were still alive."

"They were, but at least one, I'd hazard the husband, must've been shot up real bad. There's a lot of blood on the floor and under the rear seat. If you look close you can see the pattern has a section in its center where the blood is much less thick, or there's none at all. That indicates a body was lyin' there. I'd say the husband shoved his wife under the seat, they lay over her to protect her from the gunfire. He was still alive, but all shot up, when the killers pulled him and his wife from the stage. Make sense to you?"

"It does. The coroner's report said the husband was shot eight times, not countin' the bullet he put into his own brain. His wife was shot only once, in the chest, at point-blank range. There were powder burns on her dress and the flesh around the bullet hole. Her husband still had a two shot Derringer in his hand. It appears he had it hidden in his sleeve. He knew he was dying, and also knew what would happen to his wife at the hands of the gang. So he killed her. They might've planned that from the start, if they realized the danger of travelin' by stage way out here."

"You're becoming a better lawman every day, Jonas. Good work."

"*Muchas gracias.* Coming from you that means a lot. So what do we do next?"

"We go back to the post. I want to look over those reports. Soon as that's done, we stock up on supplies for a long trip. We're headed to the site of that holdup."

"Do you really believe you can find any clues after all this time?"

"Not just clues, but also a trail. I understand, even though you got caught in a storm, it hasn't rained down this way for weeks. And, despite what most people believe, rain doesn't wash out tracks all that easy. I've been able to pick up a trail even after a real frog strangler of a storm. So we're ridin' out this afternoon. Only thing we're not doin' is tellin' anyone where we're headed. That includes the sheriff, marshal, and their deputies, too. There's always the possibility some alleged upright, outstanding citizen, including a local lawman, is in cahoots with this bunch. If anyone asks, we're just goin' out and scoutin' around. Taking a *pasear* around the countryside. Let's tell Daraj we're finished here and be on our way."

16

Will and Jonas rode until shortly after sundown, then made camp for the night. They were up and in their saddles again by first light. They reached the location of the Dallas to Albuquerque stage holdup just after noon.

"Even though it's been some time, and this is a busy road, you can still see some signs of the robbery," Jonas said, as they sat their horses. He reached into his saddlebags, and pulled out a sketch of the scene which one of the deputies had drawn. He looked at it, then pointed out the various details.

"The stage was found over there, where the horses had wandered to try'n pull on some grass. The driver's body was still in the seat. The guard's was found in the road, where he'd fallen from the coach. Three men were dead inside. The young couple was over on the other side of the road, lying next to each other. There are tracks where the gang came off the ridge. The sheriff and posse followed them as far as they could, but lost 'em in the *malpais*."

"*We're* gonna follow those tracks, and *we're not* gonna lose 'em," Will declared. "Count on that. Let's look around here first."

He swung out of his saddle, Jonas following his lead. They began casting back and forth, looking for sign. Will was near the spot where the young couple had fallen when he spotted something in the dust. He leaned over and picked it up.

"Jonas! I've got something over here."

Jonas hurried over to his partner.

"What've you got?"

"A human tooth. Dollars to doughnuts the woman knocked it out of an outlaw's mouth. He probably laid his hands on her, and she smacked his face, but good."

"I wouldn't bet against that," Jonas said. "Might even have been the same son of a bitch whose hair she pulled out."

"Could be. Let's look around a bit more. I doubt we'll find anything else, but let's make sure. Then we'll start trailin' this bunch."

After a few more minutes of searching, it was obvious no further clues would be found at the robbery site.

"Let's start following those tracks," Will said.

They remounted, and went to the bottom of the embankment lining the right side of the road.

"Right above here is where they waited, then came down after they shot up the stage," Will said. "It would've been impossible for them to brush out their tracks. The horses cut up the dirt and grass too much. Let's see where they take us."

They urged their horses up the steep embankment. When they reached the top, they paused to allow Pete and Rebel to blow.

"The trail's pretty clear so far," Jonas said.

"Yeah, but it won't be for much longer," Will answered. "Unless the posse members were awful bad trackers. Or the sheriff leadin' it didn't really want to find the gang."

"You think that's a possibility?"

Will shrugged his shoulders.

"*Quien sabe?*" But it wouldn't be the first time a lawman was workin' hand in glove with a criminal outfit. Let's keep moving."

After a mile, the tracks of the fleeing men's horses disappeared on hardpan, which took few impressions of the hooves of even shod, hard ridden horses.

"Here's where you get a real lesson in followin' a trail, Jonas," Will said.

"There ain't any trail to follow," Jonas objected.

"Watch and learn."

Will pushed Pete into a slow walk. He zigzagged the horse, leaning low in the saddle as he weaved Pete back and forth, looking for the most minute piece of evidence showing which way the outlaws might have gone.

"Here's something," he said. He plucked a long strand of black horsehair from an ocotillo wand.

"This came off a horse's tail. There's also a scrape on a rock just ahead, made by a horseshoe. Our boys headed this way."

"I never could've spotted those," Jonas said.

"Sure you could have," Will assured him. "It's

just a matter of learning how to observe every little thing, no matter how small. That also helps a Ranger stay alive longer. It's gonna be slow, but we'll come up with those sons of bitches, or at least where they hole up between jobs."

"Lead the way, Professor."

"Sure thing."

Another quarter mile led them to a pile of dried out horse droppings.

"We're still heading in the right direction," Will said.

They continued following the tracks of the outlaws, going by a piece of cloth caught on a cactus spine here, an upturned rock there. Patches of sandy soil yielded hoof prints, dried up mounds of human waste indicated where one of the men had stopped to relieve himself. Quite often, when even Will was about to admit he'd lost the trail, a discarded cigarette butt would bring them back to it.

"The farther along we get, the more likely it is the tracks will be easier to follow," Will said. "Men on the run almost always get careless once they've decided they've eluded any pursuers. I'd bet these are no exception. We'll be able move a lot faster before goin' too much farther. Probably sometime tomorrow. It won't be long before it'll be too dark to follow a trail, so we'll camp at the first likely spot."

"That won't be too soon for me," Jonas said. "I

dunno if my back'll ever straighten up. I'm damn tired of lookin' at the ground."

"That's another reason we'll be stoppin' soon," Will answered. "Our eyes need a break. Tired eyes miss things they shouldn't. First spring or waterhole we come to we'll call it a day."

17

The next two days proved not much easier than the first, despite Will's optimism. Keeping on the outlaws' trail proved to be hard, painstaking work. Several times they lost it, taking an hour or more to once again find a hoof print, horse droppings, or some other hint they were still on the outlaws' tails.

"The men we're after seem to have a definite place they're headed for," Jonas said. "Their tracks have been heading pretty steadily southeast from the holdup site."

"They have," Will agreed. "I've got a good idea where they're goin'. Buffalo Gap. It used to be the Taylor County seat, until the Texas and Pacific Railroad bypassed it. The county then voted to move its seat to Abilene. Buffalo Gap's kind of stagnated, withering away ever since. It'd be a good place for an outlaw bunch to make its headquarters. I've decided to stop followin' the trail and head straight there."

"That means we'll chance losing them, if they didn't go to Buffalo Gap."

"I know that, but I figure if they didn't, we'll go on to Abilene. They could have taken a round-about route to get there. We'll be comin' up on a small settlement named Border's Chapel shortly. We'll stop there for some chuck and to rest and feed the horses. Mebbe we can pick up some information there. If our men did go to Buffalo Gap, from here they'd have to ride through Border's Chapel. There's no easy way around it. And it's only about five miles outside of Buffalo Gap."

Late that afternoon the Rangers rode into Border's Chapel, which in later years would become the town of Caps. The new name was chosen during a meeting to decide what to rename the town. One of the attendees tossed his cap into the air and shouted, "Let's call it Caps." And the voters did. But when Will and Jonas rode into the town, it only consisted of a few small homes, a small store, and the ubiquitous saloon. There was also the chapel, now unused, its paint peeling and faded. The steeple tilted precariously to the left, appearing as if the next strong windstorm would topple it. Too small to even support a livery stable, the town had a small public corral where anyone could place their horses for the night, at no charge.

The few people on the street paid little attention to the newcomers, most not even giving them a second glance. Will's brown hair and eyes, along with his lean build, and Jonas, with his blonde hair, blue eyes, also lean, but two or three inches shorter than Will, were as nondescript as any other saddle tramps who came into town, then left just as quickly. Their hair and beards had grown long, the men and their horses both covered with dust. With their badges tucked away in their vest pockets, they showed no signs of being Texas Rangers. They reined up in front of the saloon, looped their horses' reins around the hitch rail, and went inside. The only person in the place was the proprietor, who was behind the bar, polishing glasses. He looked up, a bit surprised to find customers walking in this time of the day.

"Howdy, gents. Welcome to my place, which ain't even got a name. At least I do. David Hemmings, at your service. What can I get you?"

"Two beers. I'm Will, my pard's Jonas."

"Two beers, comin' right up. Five cents apiece."

Will tossed a dime on the bar.

"My pard'll get the next two. You happen to have any grub to go along with the beer?"

"I can whip up some ham and eggs, if that'll do. Twenty-five cents."

"That'll do just fine."

"I'll get to work on 'em. I reckon I'll fix some for myself and join you fellers, if you don't mind. I'm hungry myself. We don't get a lot of people passin' through here. Glad for the company."

"That's all right with us," Will said. "We'll wander over to the table in the corner."

"I'll have the grub ready right quick."

"Bring along two more beers, and one for yourself. We're buyin'," Will answered.

"Why, that's right kind of you. I'm obliged."

Hemmings went into the small kitchen out back, while Will and Jonas sat down at the table Will had indicated.

"You think he'll tell us anything?" Jonas asked. He took another swallow of his beer.

"I dunno," Will said. "It depends on how scared he is, or whether he might've been paid to keep his mouth shut. The gang might have this whole town buffaloed. Or there's still the possibility they never come here, just rode around the place."

"You mean Buffaloed Gap," Jonas said, with a laugh.

"One more joke like that and you won't live to see Buffalo Gap," Will warned him. "You won't have to worry about any outlaws gunnin' you down. I'll do it myself."

In a few minutes, Hemmings came out of the kitchen carrying three plates of scrambled eggs and ham. He placed those on the table, then went back to the bar, drew three more beers, and returned. He sat down in the sole empty chair.

"I'm not much of a cook," he admitted, "but it's easy enough to make ham and eggs without ruining 'em. Hope you enjoy them."

"We've been on the trail eatin' nothing but

bacon and beans long enough anything else is a welcome change," Will said.

"What brings you fellers to Border's Chapel, if I'm not bein' too nosy?"

"You aren't," Will assured him. "We're just passing through. Trying to catch up with some friends of ours up to Abilene. They might've passed through here."

"Friends, huh? I can tell you if they've been here recently. I don't miss anything in this town. Not that there's much to miss. How many of 'em are there?"

"We're not certain." Will said. "Some of them may have split off and gone their own way. They're kind of a fiddle-footed bunch. So there could be just two or three, or as many as a half dozen or so."

Hemmings' face grew hard. He got up, yanked the plates and mugs from in front of the Rangers.

"I knew you weren't what you were claimin' to be. Y'all belong to the Trent bunch. You know right where you're headed. So do I. To Hell, if you don't change your ways. And good riddance. Tell Luke Trent when you see him that he's sucked me dry. I'll scrape together enough money for next month's blackmail payment, but then I'm done. I'm gonna pull up stakes and move on, before he can kill me, like he's pretty much killed this town. Buffalo Gap too."

"Hold on just a minute," Will said, keeping his hands on the table to show he had no intention of going for his gun. "Who is this Luke Trent? We've never heard of him."

"You know damn well who he is."

"We damn for certain don't," Jonas said, his face flushed with anger.

"You've really never ridden with Trent and his bunch?" Hemmings asked, a trace of doubt still in his voice.

Will slid his hand into his vest pocket, took out his badge, then held it in his palm for Hemmings to see. He folded his fingers back over the badge so quickly that, for a moment, the saloon owner wasn't quite sure of what he'd seen.

"I'll swear on this we haven't. We're Texas Rangers, on the trail of a bunch of *mal hombres* who've been robbin' stages and killin' folks all over this section. We don't have a clue as to who's behind the outfit. They never leave anyone alive, and they're dang good at covering their trail. We managed to follow them from outside Sweetwater, where they held up the Dallas to Albuquerque stage, killing seven people, including a young couple from back East, to here. You can take my word for it, or not. It sounds like this Trent character you mentioned just might be who we're after. I'm taking a big chance showing you my badge. We have no way of knowin' but that you might be working as a spy for this Trent, lettin' him know whenever the law comes ridin' through here."

Hemmings swore a foul oath.

"Don't you ever accuse me of workin' for that son of a bitch," Mister."

"All right, I won't. But what can you tell me about him? Where's he hole up when he's not out robbin' and killin'?"

"Luke Trent doesn't hole up at all. He rides high, wide, and handsome. Has this town and Buffalo Gap under his thumb. Everyone in Abilene believes he's a big, successful rancher. What they don't know is he supports his ranch from money he's stolen. He has a big spread three miles east of here. The Circle T. Entrance is marked by a fancy wrought iron gate. The house and bunkhouse is a half mile beyond that. I'm signing my death warrant by tellin' you fellers this."

Will attempted to reassure him.

"No, you're not. Me'n Jonas are gonna take that bunch down. They'll be out of business for good."

"Just the two of you? Against the entire Trent gang?"

"Those odds sound about right. How many men does Trent have ridin' with him?"

"Usually seven. Trent himself, then Pasco Lawton is his second-in-command."

"I've heard of Lawton," Jonas said. "He's a real

bad one. He's on the Ranger's Fugitive List, for killing four men over in El Paso. Last we knew he was still in New Mexico Territory,"

"Not no more he ain't. The others are Sam "Smitty" Smith, Joe Barnes, Hank Dawkins, Dan Bell, and Ed Carruthers. I know all of them because they come over once a month to collect Trent's 'protection' money and soak up all the liquor they can, without payin' me a dime, of course. All hard men to deal with."

"We're used to handling their kind," Will said. "We'll head out there right now. I hope you aren't planning on double-crossing us. If word gets to Trent we're on our way, that'll sign *our* death warrants."

"Ranger, I've been livin' like a slave on an old plantation ever since Trent took over this territory. If you bring him to an end, that'll give me back my independence. That's all I want. I'm too old and scared to fight and too tired to run."

"Any women about the place? We don't want to hurt them if there are?"

Hemmings shook his head.

"Not unless they brought some of the gals from the Little Palace of Pleasure in Buffalo Gap home with 'em."

Other cowboys or wranglers?"

"Nope. Trent claims to be a rancher, but there ain't a cow on the place. He says he's waitin' on some special breeding stock to arrive from

England. Let me tell you, those cows are either on the slowest boat you can imagine, or the damn thing's sunk. I still say you're plumb loco, just the two of you goin' after Trent and his men."

"Then we'll try our best," Will said. "That'll have to do. If we're not back by tomorrow evening, then you'll know we're dead, so in that case you'd better make a break for it. C'mon, Jonas, let's go. There's no sense in putting this off."

"One more question Will didn't ask," Jonas said. "Do any of those men happen to be a redhead?"

"That'd be Smitty Smith. Brightest red hair I've ever seen on anyone, outside of a saloon gal's henna dyed locks."

"Places him at the scene, Will."

"One more nail in the gang's coffin. Let's get after them. We don't want to lose them now that we're so close to roundin' up the entire bunch."

"You haven't finished your meal," Hemmings pointed out.

"A wise doctor told me some time back, if you're headin' into a gunfight, do it on an empty stomach." Will said. "If you take a bullet in your guts, you're more likely to survive if there's nothin' in 'em. So we go in with empty bellies but full guns. We're obliged for the information. You just made our job a lot easier. *Hasta la vista*."

"*Adios*. May the Good Lord protect y'all."

18

"How are we gonna handle this, Will?" Jonas asked, as they neared the Circle T.

"We're just goin' straight on in, yell for those bastards to give themselves up, and when they don't, start shootin'. Sound simple enough?"

"Well, yeah, if we want to get our brains blown out. You're not gonna wait until after sundown, and try'n sneak in there once it's full dark?"

"No. Too many things could go wrong. They know the setup of the place. We don't. We need to be able to see what we're up against. It'd also be too easy for at least some of the bunch to get past us in the dark, and head for parts unknown. Or for one of us to mistake the other for an outlaw. So we go in now."

This part of Texas was mostly flat to rolling plains, but there were sections of low hills and mesas. This area was one of them. Trent's Circle T Ranch was nestled between two of those.

"We could try'n get to the top, take the high ground," Jonas suggested.

"That might work, but they've got plenty of food and water, while we don't," Will said. "They could simply wait us out. There's the entrance just ahead. Time to take out our rifles."

They pulled their Winchesters from the saddle

scabbards, checking them to make certain they were loaded and ready.,

"There don't seem to be any guards. Soon as we go through the gate, we'll shout and rouse those *hombres*, then duck for cover," Will said. "I'd hazard they're all in the bunkhouse, except for Trent and mebbe Lawton. You take that, I'll take the main house. I don't need to tell you we're dealin' with cold-blooded killers, so don't hesitate to shoot any down that you get in your sights."

"Boy howdy, you don't have to worry about that," Jonas said. "Let's get this done."

They walked their horses through the gate. Will cupped his hands around his mouth and called out.

"Y'all in the house, and the bunkhouse. Texas Rangers! Y'all are wanted for murder and robbery, plus other charges. Come out with your hands in the air, and no weapons. Right now!"

It only took a moment for Will to receive his answer. Glass shattered as rifle barrels poked through the windows of both buildings. He and Jonas rolled from their saddles, sending Pete and Rebel back through the gate to safety.

Will ducked behind a wood pile. Jonas found shelter behind a large rock, which seemed to serve no purpose, other than being too large to easily remove. Outlaw bullets plowed into the logs and rock, sending splinters of wood and chips of rock flying in all directions. Some of the slugs ricocheted wildly, but none made a hit on their intended targets.

One of the men in the bunkhouse's face and shoulders showed as he attempted a shot. Jonas popped up, fired once, then ducked back behind the boulder. His bullet caught Dan Bell just below the junction of his throat and chest, splintering the collarbone, sending fragments into his windpipe. Bell dropped, gasping for breath that would not come.

Will made a mad dash across the yard. He rolled onto the porch of the main house, drawing the fire of the men in the bunkhouse. He dove against the wall and huddled there, as bullets tore into the house, breaking off bits of stucco.

Jonas kept Will covered, then ran to the wood pile where Will had sheltered. He stopped for just a moment, then shot the bunkhouse door off its hinges. He reloaded, ran to the bunkhouse, dove to his belly, and opened fire. Joe Barnes went down with a bullet in his chest, just under his left nipple. A bullet from Hank Dawkins's six-gun tore a bloody groove along the right side of Jonas's head, from his temple to above the ear. Jonas's return shots took Dawkins in the right side of his chest and belly, spinning him to the floor. Ed Carruthers, panicked at seeing his partners all dead or dying, tried to make a run out the back door. Jonas put a bullet into the back of his skull, Carruthers stumbled, then fell, hauling up against a wall. There was no one else in the building.

The situation at the main house was at a standstill, Will pinned down, but the men inside unable to move with the certainty of knowing if they showed themselves, they'd receive a Ranger bullet for their trouble.

Jonas walked to the bunkhouse door.

"Y'all in the house," he called. "All your men are dead. I suggest you come out before the same happens to you."

"Not a chance," came the answer.

"Then suit yourselves."

Once again, Jonas riddled the door with lead, until this one also fell from its hinges.

Will jumped up and crashed through the window, taking the three men in the house off guard. They'd expected him to come through the door. Only Pasco Lawton got off a shot, which burned along Will's left side before he dropped all three of them. Smitty Smith was shot in the forehead, blood as red as his fiery hair spurting from the hole. Before Lawton could fire again, Will shot him through the center of his gut. Lawton doubled over and slumped to the floor. His Winchester now empty, Will tossed it aside and pulled his Peacemaker from its holster.

Luke Trent was the hardest to kill. Will had to empty his Colt into the big man before he went down, putting three bullets diagonally into Trent's stomach, two in his right breast, and one into the center of his chest. Trent stood for a moment, shuddering, then crumpled.

"It's all over, Jonas," Will shouted, as he scrambled to his feet. "You all right?"

While he waited for Jonas, Will checked the men he'd gunned down. Only Lawton was still breathing, but wouldn't be for long. Smith was lying with his mouth agape, a gap in his upper front teeth indicating he was indeed the man who'd lost his tooth during the stage robbery. There was a chunk of his hair missing, red hair which matched the hank Will had in his saddlebags.

"Jonas, where are you? You hurt?" Will called again.

"I'm here."

Jonas appeared in the doorway, a vacuous expression on his face, a wild look in his eyes.

"Jonas?"

"Looks like you're the last renegade left," Jonas muttered. "Time for you to die, you female-murderin' son of a bitch."

He lifted his Smith and Wesson, aimed it right at Will's stomach.

"Jonas, no. It's me, Will, your partner."

Jonas thumbed back the hammer of his revolver.

"Jonas, no! Don't do this!" Will pleaded.

Jonas pulled the trigger.

Center Point Large Print
600 Brooks Road / PO Box 1
Thorndike, ME 04986-0001 USA

(207) 568-3717

US & Canada:
1 800 929-9108
www.centerpointlargeprint.com